She I
And Tha

He caught a perfumed whiff of her dark, shoulder-length hair as she strode by him.

"You are definitely in need of help." She handed him her business card and turned to the door.

He glanced down at the card, then followed her out to the elevator. "Wait a second. Dose this mean you're taking the job?"

She pushed the button. "Yes."

"But...when will you start?"

The elevator dinged and the doors opened. She stepped inside. "Right away."

"But how do we do this? If you're going to be my bodyguard, shouldn't you be staying here? Where are you going?"

As she pushed the down button inside the elevator, a tiny infectious grin sneaked across her lips. "I liked the look of those feathery pillows in your guest room, Dr. Knight, so if you must know, I'm going to get my toothbrush and jammies."

The doors closed in front of Donovan's face.

He stood in the vestibule holding her card, feeling transfixed and suddenly exuberant, and totally surprised by the fact that his cool, reserved bodyguard actually had a sense of humor.

Things were definitely going to get interesting around here.

Dear Reader,

Top off your summer reading list with six brand-new steamy romances from Silhouette Desire!

Reader favorite Ann Major brings the glamorous LONE STAR COUNTRY CLUB miniseries into Desire with *Shameless* (#1513). This rancher's reunion romance is the first of three titles set in Mission Creek, Texas—where society reigns supreme and appearances are everything. Next, our exciting yearlong series DYNASTIES: THE BARONES continues with *Beauty & the Blue Angel* (#1514) by Maureen Child, in which a dashing naval hero goes overboard for a struggling mom-to-be.

Princess in His Bed (#1515) by *USA TODAY* bestselling author Leanne Banks is the third Desire title in her popular miniseries THE ROYAL DUMONTS. Enjoy the fun as a tough Wyoming rancher loses his heart to a spirited royal-in-disguise. Next, a brooding horseman shows a beautiful rancher the ropes...of desire in *The Gentrys: Abby* (#1516) by Linda Conrad.

In the latest BABY BANK title, *Marooned with a Millionaire* (#1517) by Kristi Gold, passion ignites between a powerful hotel magnate and the pregnant balloonist stranded on his yacht. And a millionaire M.D. brings out the temptress in his tough-girl bodyguard in *Sleeping with the Playboy* (#1518) by veteran Harlequin Historicals and debut Desire author Julianne MacLean.

Get your summer off to a sizzling start with six new passionate, powerful and provocative love stories from Silhouette Desire.

Enjoy!

Melissa Jeglinski
Senior Editor, Silhouette Desire

Please address questions and book requests to:
Silhouette Reader Service
U.S.: 3010 Walden Ave., P.O. Box 1325, Buffalo, NY 14269
Canadian: P.O. Box 609, Fort Erie, Ont. L2A 5X3

Sleeping with the Playboy

JULIANNE MacLEAN

Published by Silhouette Books
America's Publisher of Contemporary Romance

SILHOUETTE BOOKS

ISBN 0-373-76518-5

SLEEPING WITH THE PLAYBOY

Copyright © 2003 by Julianne MacLean

Visit Silhouette at www.eHarlequin.com

Printed in U.S.A.

JULIANNE MacLEAN

Before embarking on the wonderful challenge of writing romance, Julianne earned degrees in both English literature and business administration. She spent some time as a financial statement auditor, but is now wildly happy to be a full-time mom and romance writer. She lives in Nova Scotia, Canada, with her husband and five-year-old daughter. Julianne loves to hear from readers, and invites you to visit her Web site at www.juliannemaclean.com.

A thousand thank-yous to a writer's dream editor,
Melissa Endlich.

One

Here we go—trotting into someone else's world again. Jocelyn Mackenzie followed her client out of the mahogany-paneled elevator and across the marble vestibule, to the double doors of the ritzy Chicago penthouse. She glanced up at the crystal chandelier overhead and the modern steel sculpture against the side wall, and felt the familiar onslaught of awe.

Not that she hadn't seen her share of fancy penthouses and stone mansions. To be honest, that's where she usually took assignments as a bodyguard, because quite simply, the average Joe couldn't afford her.

It was for reasons of her own, however, that she would never choose this kind of lavish, pretentious lifestyle for herself.

The elevator doors slid closed behind them, and Dr. Reeves knocked on the door. Jocelyn waited beside him, hands clasped at her back, curious as to how her potential "principal" would answer. Would he open the door without asking who it was, or would he use the optical viewer?

The crystal knob turned, and the door swung open. She'd have to educate her client about that.

Before she could give that another thought, however, Jocelyn found herself gazing up at a handsome, golden-haired gentleman dressed in a tuxedo, his starched, white shirt unbuttoned at the neck, his black bow tie undone and dangling in front. Slender and strong, tall and confident, with just the right mixture of arrogance and appeal, he was alarmingly, heart-stoppingly gorgeous.

This was a man who belonged on the cover of *GQ* magazine—a man who made Jocelyn's breath stop and twirl around in her throat. Before she realized it, she'd taken a stupefied step back.

Good God, what was wrong with her? This was a business call.

Sweeping her feminine instincts out of her head and summoning more professional ones, she surmised that this wealthy doctor undoubtedly had his share of obsessed lovers. Potential stalkers were probably where she should begin if his case was typical.

The man's green eyes warmed at the sight of Dr. Reeves, then his gaze moved leisurely to Jocelyn and settled on her face.

"Mark, what are you doing here?" he asked, looking at Jocelyn, not Mark. His voice was calm, but there was an underlying sensuality as he watched Jocelyn, a tone that warned her right off that he was a flirt.

Why wouldn't he be? Most women would probably fall at his feet for a single moment's pleasure of being the object of that fiery gaze.

She chastised herself again. *He's a client, Jocelyn. Those thoughts should not even be in your brain.*

Still holding the door open, he backed up a step. "Come in."

Dr. Reeves gestured for Jocelyn to enter first. She stepped inside, her loafers hushed by the oriental rug as she took in the style of the penthouse—the marble floors, the Grecian columns and the sheer square-footage and height of the ceilings. Classical music played softly from the living room just ahead of her, where the lighting was dim and restful. A glass of red wine had been placed on the coffee table. An open, hard-covered book lay beside it.

Jocelyn looked up at another enormous crystal chandelier over her head in the center of the foyer, then pulled her gaze down and held out her hand. "Dr. Knight, I'm Jocelyn Mackenzie."

He hesitated a moment, then shook it. "It's a pleasure to meet you." He looked over her shoulder at Dr. Reeves. "What's this all about?"

Jocelyn turned. Dr. Reeves, the man who had retained her to be Dr. Knight's bodyguard for the indeterminable future, fumbled for an answer. The two doctors stared at each other for a second or two.

Oh, no. "He's not expecting us?" she asked Dr. Reeves.

"Should I be?"

Jocelyn felt her temper begin to rise. She didn't like being misled, nor did she wish to work for anyone who wasn't absolutely in need of her help. In *desperate* need. She had been under the impression that Dr. Knight was anxious for her to begin. His friend, Dr. Reeves, had told her about the intruder who'd broken into this penthouse a few nights ago, and the threatening letter that had come the next day.

Hell, she'd already done the advance breakdowns on Dr. Knight's parking garage, the hospital where he worked and his regular route to and from.

"Now, wait a second, let me explain," Dr. Reeves said.

"Explain what?" her principal replied.

Jocelyn shook her head and stared at the man who'd hired her. "He's waiting, Dr. Reeves, and frankly so am I."

"What the hell's going on here?"

Dr. Reeves raised his hands. "Calm down, both of you. Donovan, I wanted you to meet Ms. Mackenzie before you said no."

"Said no to what?" He took in Jocelyn's full appearance, from her starched white shirt and brown blazer, down the length of her pants to her brown leather shoes. "Who are you?"

Jocelyn squared her shoulders. "I've been hired to be your bodyguard, Dr. Knight, but I was under the impression you wanted one."

"A bodyguard? Mark, you had no right—"

"I had every right. You're my partner and I'm not about to lose you and have to cover all our patients while you're laid up or dead. I'd be on call 24-7, and that was never how we intended to run our practice." Dr. Reeves's cheeks colored. "Besides, I'm worried about you, buddy."

The two men stood in silence, as if neither was sure what to say to the other.

"Maybe I should leave," Jocelyn said. "You two

can discuss this, and when you've got it figured out, you can call me, though I can't guarantee I'll be available.'' She turned to go, wishing she had taken Congressman Jenkin's request instead.

Dr. Reeves grabbed her arm as she tried to pass. ''Ms. Mackenzie, please wait.''

Jocelyn glanced down at his hand, tight around her elbow, then sent him a warning look.

He immediately released her.

''Dr. Knight needs your services, and his patients need him. Chicago can't afford to lose its best heart surgeon, nor can I lose a friend.''

She shook her head. ''It's his choice, not yours. I need cooperation from my clients. They have to be willing and eager to work with me and take the situation seriously. Without that kind of commitment from the people I work with, I walk.''

She tried to leave again. Dr. Reeves followed her into the vestibule. Jocelyn pressed the elevator button.

''Please, I'm begging you,'' Dr. Reeves said. ''Stay and check things out. See what you can do for him.''

''Why is it *you're* the one out here begging me, and not him?'' She gestured toward the open door of the penthouse, where Dr. Knight was still standing in the foyer, looking as relaxed as ever, watching.

''I can convince him.'' Dr. Reeves took a desperate step toward his friend. ''Donovan, you need her. You can't put yourself in danger like this. Your patients need you and your penthouse needs a security system. The police don't have time to give your case the attention it needs, and I sure as hell am not going to lose any more sleep worrying about you.''

"I'll change my locks."

"That's not enough. If this attacker is determined, he'll be back. Besides…" Dr. Reeves lowered his voice. "Think of the Counseling Center. You're almost there, buddy, and it means everything to you. You can't take these kinds of risks with your life, nor can you give the project what it needs if you're checking over your shoulder every five minutes. You need to finish what you started."

A long silence ensued. Jocelyn had the impression Dr. Reeves had touched a nerve with that Counseling Center argument, whatever that was about.

Jocelyn pressed the elevator button again, and Dr. Reeves returned to her. "Please, Ms. Mackenzie, don't go."

"You should have discussed this with Dr. Knight before you called me out here and wasted my time. I have a long waiting list of people who need and want my help, and this is not—"

"How long a waiting list?" Dr. Knight asked, moving forward to stand in the open doorway. He leaned a broad shoulder against the doorjamb.

Both Jocelyn and Dr. Reeves faced him in silence.

He had way of halting a conversation just by entering into it, Jocelyn thought as she stared at him in a studious kind of way. She had the most intense desire to know what he was thinking.

God, he was gorgeous.

"Long enough," she replied.

"So you're that good?"

"She's the best," Dr. Reeves replied. "She used to be in the Secret Service. She has a list of references a mile long. Very *impressive* references, Donovan."

Dr. Knight stepped out of the doorway and sauntered leisurely toward her. Jocelyn's senses became
acutely alert as he grew closer and closer, and she
fought the urge to take another step back.

She fought also to understand that self-preserving
urge, for he was in no way threatening. Predatory,
yes, in a sexual kind of way, when she suspected he
was not trying to be sexual. That particular aspect of
his demeanor seemed to come naturally; it was an
unconscious part of him.

Maybe that's why she found him threatening.

"Why did you leave the Secret Service?" he
asked. "You weren't fired, were you?"

Now he was insulting her. "No, I wasn't fired. The
money's better in this racket."

Money, as it happened, was something she needed
a great deal of right now.

He nodded. "I take it you know how to use that
Glock." He glanced down at the gun she wore inside
her jacket.

"I can drop you on your ass with it, Dr. Knight,
and that's without pulling the trigger."

He inclined his head at her and said nothing for a
long moment. She guessed he was taking his turn at
being studious.

The elevator dinged and the doors opened. No one
moved. Dr. Knight continued to gaze at her, waiting
to see what she would do. For a moment or two, they
all stood in the gleaming vestibule while the elevator
waited.

Then the doors quietly closed, and the lighted buttons went dark.

Jocelyn sensed Dr. Reeves' heavy sigh of relief.

"I'd like to know how you work," Dr. Knight

said. "Then I'll decide whether or not I can commit."

Jocelyn raised an eyebrow. She almost laughed. "I'm afraid it's going to be the other way around, Dr. Knight. *I'll* be the one to ask the questions, then *I'll* decide if I want to commit."

To her surprise, Dr. Knight smiled at Dr. Reeves. "You've checked out her references?"

"Of course."

"Good, because I think I like her."

Dr. Reeves sighed again. "I figured you would."

Jocelyn leaned forward in the plush, white, over-stuffed armchair. "So you think the intruder had a key, Dr. Knight?"

"Yes. He was already inside when I returned home from the opera three nights ago, and the door was locked as usual when I came in. He must have wanted me to think everything was normal, so he'd have the element of surprise on his side."

The doctor crossed one long leg over the other and took a sip of his red wine. Jocelyn had to resist staring at what was obviously a beautiful, muscled thigh under those black tuxedo trousers.

"Possibly." Jocelyn noted the details in her Palm Pilot.

"And call me Donovan."

Jocelyn didn't glance up. She merely nodded. "Is that how you got that mark on your knuckle?"

Donovan looked at the tiny laceration, no more than a quarter of an inch long. "You're very observant, Ms. Mackenzie. Yes. I got in a few good swings before he gave up whatever he was looking for and took off."

"And what do *you* think he was looking for?"

He shrugged. "That night, the police concluded it was a burglary. They said keys can be stolen easily enough, an imprint made in a matter of minutes. I've often left my keys in my lab coat pocket at the hospital while I grab a bite to eat, or misplaced them every so often."

"Doesn't everyone?" Dr. Reeves offered helpfully.

Jocelyn didn't crack a smile. "I don't. And if I take this case, Dr. Knight, the first thing I'm going to do is work on getting you out of habits like those."

Donovan's brow furrowed. "You've *never* lost your keys?"

"Not since I was in high school."

"You've never left your purse anywhere? Forgotten a credit card in a store?"

"Never."

Donovan set his wineglass down on the wrought iron end table. "You must be a detail-oriented person."

"I'm an everything person. I value my security."

"Hence your career choice." He gave her a probing look that told her he wanted to know more about her career choice and why she was what she was.

Jocelyn shrugged. She wasn't about to give him the how's and why's of her life. She had her reasons and they were her own. Besides that, she made it a rule not to divulge personal things about herself that cultivated a familiarity with her clients. She asked *them* the questions. It was entirely a one-way street, and she liked it that way.

That was the "hence" in her career choice.

"Dr. Reeves told me a threatening letter came the next day," she said.

"Yes, the police have it. It said, 'You deserve to die.'"

"Do you have any enemies, Dr. Knight?"

"Donovan. No, not that I can think of."

"Any medical malpractice suits against you? In the past or pending?"

"No."

"And it was definitely a man who attacked you? You're sure of that, even though the intruder wore a ski mask?"

"I'm sure. Why? You look like you don't believe that."

Not the least bit concerned with what he thought she believed or didn't believe, Jocelyn continued to take notes on her Palm Pilot. "I like to ask questions, Dr. Knight. Cover everything."

"Donovan," he repeated more forcefully. "Do you have a problem with first names?"

She stopped her note taking and looked directly at him. Perfection. His face was completely flawless. And damn her eyes for noticing. *Again.* "I don't have any problem with first names, Dr. Knight. Do you have a problem with *last* names?"

He watched her for a moment, then the tension in his face broke, and he smiled—the most sensual, sexy, flirtatious smile she'd ever seen in her life. His eyes flashed and he exuded an almost tangible charisma.

A hot current tingled through Jocelyn's veins. She clenched her jaw and worked hard to throttle the vexing sensation. What was wrong with her tonight? She was a professional. A damn good one.

He took another sip of wine.

Jocelyn turned her attention to Donovan's partner, because she couldn't bear another second of those olive-green eyes moving over her in that disarming way, studying her. She was not an open book, nor did she wish to feel like one. Neither did she appreciate her hormones behaving like she was back in high school. She had thought life experience had taught her to be stronger than that.

"Dr. Reeves, do you know of anyone who would want to hurt Dr. Knight?"

He shook his head. "Could be anyone. Donovan has a lot of...female acquaintances."

Jocelyn nodded, getting the picture. "Perhaps the man was a jealous lover or a husband of one of Dr. Knight's 'acquaintances.'" She turned back to Donovan. "Have you had any threats or meetings with anyone like that?"

"Hey, wait a second here. I don't have *that* many acquaintances, and certainly not ones with husbands, jealous or otherwise. Mark, you're making me out to be some kind of sex addict."

"No, not at all," Dr. Reeves replied, holding up his hands. "I just want to make sure we have all the bases covered."

Jocelyn interrupted and spoke in a professional, detached voice. "I'm not judging you, Dr. Knight. To tell you the truth, I don't really care if you're a sex addict or a gigolo or a Chippendales model on the weekends for that matter. I just want to know who would want to break into your home, and how I can prevent it from happening again. Now, I would appreciate it if you would just answer my questions honestly and stop worrying about what I think of you.''

He set down his wineglass. Looking almost amused, he inclined his head at her. ''I truly believe you *don't* care, Ms. Mackenzie, and that, oddly enough, is what makes me want to hire you.''

What did he mean by that?

He glanced at his friend. ''You chose well, Mark. Even if I didn't ask for your help.''

''I knew you'd see the light,'' Dr. Reeves replied.

Donovan stood. ''I'd like you to start right away, Ms. Mackenzie. Tonight as a matter of fact.''

Jocelyn raised her eyebrow at him again. ''When I start—*if* I start—Dr. Knight, is entirely up to me. I'll take a look around and ask some more questions first, then, and only then, will I consider taking your case. So you might as well sit back down and think back to every woman you've been with in the past six months. Then we'll talk about a retainer.''

Dr. Knight smiled again, and quite agreeably sat down.

She was the rudest, coldest, least friendly woman he had encountered since he'd finished medical school ten years ago. And she was completely irresistible.

After Mark left, Donovan followed Jocelyn into his bedroom while she examined the door that led out onto the rooftop terrace. She tried to stick a finger into the gap between the door and the frame.

''This needs to be reinforced. It should be less than one-sixteenth of an inch, or a pry bar could be slipped in and the door worked open. And you could use some more floodlights on your terrace.'' She tapped the glass. "Is this shatterproof?"

He nodded, and listened attentively to all her comments and suggestions, all the while thinking about how long it had been since a woman had spoken to him with such disinterest.

Because of his profession and his wealth—a good deal of which was inherited from his parents—women pasted on exaggerated smiles and laughed a little too long at his jokes. They generally dressed to kill, showing off cleavage and wearing spiky heels and glittery lipstick when they were in his company. The women in his life were predictable. They always had that ''Maybe I can be the future Mrs. Dr. Knight'' look in their eyes. Over the past few years, that kind of social life had begun to grow tiresome.

Jocelyn Mackenzie was different, though. She wore a plain brown suit with flat shoes, and practically no makeup. Not that she needed any. Her face had a natural beauty with healthy, rosy cheeks, full, moist lips and huge dark eyes a man could lose himself in.

She didn't give him that flirtatious look, either, batting her lashes at him. Hell, she barely even noticed him. She was more interested in the nooks and crannies of his penthouse where there were flaws in the security, and figuring out how best to fix those flaws. She didn't want to impress him. She didn't care if she pissed him off.

It was a refreshing change, to be sure.

"So tell me, Ms. Mackenzie, is my penthouse in bad shape security-wise?"

She glanced around the bedroom, her face serious, her gaze going everywhere. She eyed the mahogany,

king-size bed and the cream-colored, down-filled duvet, the black-and-white photographs on the wall; she
glanced at his dresser with his wallet lying open on
top of it, loose change from his pockets scattered all
around.

"There's always room for improvement," she replied, still in that disinterested tone. She moved to
the door, wiggled the doorknob and tried the lock.

"You're being vague, now. Are you going to
transform me, or not?"

She turned around to touch and inspect the door-
jamb. "I don't transform people."

"No, but you said you were going to break me of
some bad habits. I think I might enjoy that."

She gave him an unimpressed look. "Like leaving
your keys places. If you leave the toilet seat up, that's
your problem."

He followed her out to the kitchen. She glanced
quickly at the stainless steel appliances, the butcher's
block in the center and the white custom cabinetry.

He would've given his eyeteeth to know what she
was thinking. He could see the wheels turning in her
head as she sized up his penthouse before she decided if she wanted to take this case.

"Do you have any hired help?" she asked.

"Yeah, I have a housekeeper who comes in every
morning through the week."

She walked down the hall and returned to the
foyer, then faced him. She was petite, but there was
a strength in her that she emitted like perfume. He
wondered what kind of personal life she led. He
glanced down at her hands. No wedding ring.

Some deep male instinct in him rejoiced.

"First of all, whether we work together or not,"

she said, "I would recommend updating your alarm system. The one you have is at least fifteen years old. It's a dinosaur."

"Done."

"And you need to *use* the system. Half the people who have them installed can't be bothered punching in the codes, so they leave them inactive."

Donovan smiled. "I'm guilty of that, I'm afraid."

"I figured you were." She moved to the front door to gaze out the peephole. "Are you looking for round-the-clock management and surveillance, Dr. Knight, or just improvements to your home security?"

"I think Mark had a round-the-clock bodyguard in mind."

She faced him. "I asked what *you* wanted, Dr. Knight."

He thought about the baseball bat under his bed, and how he'd stared at the ceiling for six hours last night, then fallen asleep on his lunch hour today.

Then he thought about what his twenty-four-hour-a-day bodyguard would look like in a nightie. If she wore one. Negligee maybe? He could picture her in a red one....

"I think round-the-clock management might be beneficial—at least for the short term."

She nodded, then quietly returned to the living room. Touching a long slender finger to the book he was reading that lay open on the coffee table, she raised her eyebrows as she gazed over the page. "Triathlons."

"You look surprised."

She shrugged. "I was expecting it to be about art history or something." She moved across the room and knelt on the white sofa, to pull the ivory-colored shears back to examine the windows.

Donovan watched her reflection in the clean, dark panes. She flicked a latch.

As she reached up to try a higher latch, her jacket lifted and pulled tight around her shoulder blades, and he could see that she had a shapely behind, trim and firm beneath her loose, wool dress pants. He found himself wondering what kind of panties she wore. He suspected they'd be white. Probably cotton. Maybe silk.

"I'm not much interested in art history," he said distractedly, watching her return to her feet and smooth out her clothes.

She ignored him, and that intrigued him even more. He caught a perfumy whiff of her dark, shoulder-length hair as she strode by him.

A few minutes later, they were back in the foyer and she was reaching into her breast pocket for a business card. She gazed directly into his eyes. "You are *definitely* in need of help."

She handed him the card, and turned to the door.

He glanced down at the card, then followed her out to the elevator. "Wait a second. Does this mean you're taking the job?"

She pushed the button. "Yes."

"But…when will you start?"

The elevator dinged and the doors opened. She stepped inside. "Right away."

"But how do we do this? If you're going to be my bodyguard, shouldn't you be staying here? Where are you going?"

As she pushed the down button inside the elevator, a tiny infectious grin sneaked across her lips. "I liked the look of those feathery pillows in your guest room, Dr. Knight, so if you must know, I'm going to get my toothbrush and jammies.''

The doors closed in front of Donovan's face.

He stood in the vestibule holding her card, feeling transfixed and suddenly exuberant, and totally surprised by the fact that his cool, reserved bodyguard actually had a sense of humor.

Things were definitely going to get interesting around here.

Two

Jocelyn grabbed hold of the brass handrail in the elevator, then tipped her head back and tapped it three times, hard against the oak-paneled wall.

What in God's name had possessed her to say such a stupid, suggestive thing? She was a professional, dammit, and she had a well-deserved reputation for objective, serious behavior and an almost masculine demeanor that demanded respect from the world of executive protection. She *never* smiled at clients. Not unless they made a joke and etiquette required it. Never was *she* the one to make the joke. And certainly not a sexual one!

She reached the bottom floor and stepped off the elevator into the lobby. The uniformed gentleman at the security desk nodded at her as she passed by.

A few minutes later, she was walking down the dark street to where her car was parked, debating whether or not she should have taken this job. She didn't approve of rich, snobby doctors—especially gorgeous ones who wore tuxedos and went to the opera and ballet just to add polish to their appearance, and expected every female within spitting distance to dissolve into a puddle of infatuation at their feet.

It was all so pretentious, and she hated that kind of thing. She had her reasons, of course. And okay, maybe they were personal, but what had happened in her life *happened,* and she'd experienced firsthand the kind of shallow pomposity people like Dr. Knight were capable of.

Besides her father—who had left his own, personal imprint on her as a woman—she'd experienced the social-climbing doctor type. The type who went to medical school just to get a summer home on Rhode Island, a yacht moored at the most prestigious club and a Mercedes parked in a three-car garage.

A Mercedes. All through medical school, Tom had talked about getting one. He'd lovingly referred to his future purchase as "The Merc."

Jocelyn pushed those memories aside and pulled out her cell phone. She called her assistant, Tess, to tell her she'd be taking the assignment. She then retrieved her overnight bag from the trunk of her 1987 Acura Legend, and headed back to Dr. Knight's high-rise, wondering if it wasn't too late to back out, and how she could go about doing that. Because, despite everything she'd just told herself about how much she hated pretentious men who wielded their wealth like swords dipped in liquid aphrodisiac, she had responded to the bold, sexy look in Dr. Knight's eyes. The sheer perfection of his face and the sensual way he'd walked as he'd followed her around his penthouse, so relaxed and casual about everything, had made her feel uncomfortably hot beneath her starchy, cotton blouse. She'd had to work hard to keep her eyes to herself and concentrate on her job, and she wasn't used to distractions like that.

Perhaps she could tell him that her assistant had just called to inform her that her previous principal wanted her to return for another month.

But that would be lying, and she really hated people who lied.

Surely she could handle this.

Deciding to at least give Dr. Knight's case some time—it would be a hefty paycheck after all, and she wanted to cover her sister's university tuition—Jocelyn returned to his building and purposefully didn't stop at the security desk to check in. The guard didn't say a word. Sure, he might have already seen her come and go once, but that wasn't good enough for her. She pulled out her Palm Pilot and made note of it, then while she rode the elevator up, checked the red emergency phone, just to make sure it worked.

Donovan leaned back against the kitchen counter and took a sip of his beer. What had he been thinking, hiring a woman on the spot to move into his place and be his bodyguard? His bodyguard!

He should have given it more thought. He usually didn't make decisions on the spur of the moment, unless they were medical emergencies and circumstances demanded it. When it came to his personal life, he preferred to take three days to mull over a decision, just to make sure he wasn't acting impulsively.

Which in this case, he most certainly was.

Damn Mark for bringing up the Counseling Center. Mark knew Donovan too well—knew he wouldn't be able to say no after that. The Center was, after all, the most important thing in his life these days, and he wanted to see it through to the end. A security expert was definitely a sensible idea.

Sensible indeed. While his "expert" had been wandering around the penthouse poking her nose everywhere, all he'd been able to think about was what she would look like naked.

Unfortunately, that last bit weighed a little too heavily in the decision-making process. What could he say? He was a man, and the idea of sharing his penthouse with an attractive woman who didn't seem to *want* something from him was an appealing notion. It hadn't been entirely about her skill as a security expert, though she certainly seemed competent enough, and as much as he'd initially denied it to Mark, he did feel the need for hired protection.

To give himself credit, though, he supposed his decision was something his gut had played a part in. Somehow he'd sensed that Jocelyn Mackenzie was knowledgeable about security and more than capable, and for reasons he couldn't quite explain, he felt comfortable trusting her—which was a novel concept for Donovan.

The doorbell rang, and he carried his beer with him to answer it.

"That's the second time you did that," Jocelyn said as soon as their eyes met.

"Did what?"

"You opened the door without using the optical viewer."

"The peephole? I knew it was you."

"How?"

"I knew you were coming right back." He stepped aside to invite her in.

"I could have been anybody. And your security guard downstairs isn't a hundred percent reliable, by the way. I'll deal with that tomorrow, after a few more tests."

"Tests? What kind of tests?"

"I'm just going to see how easy it is to get by." With a large, black tote bag slung over her shoulder, she waited in the center of the foyer while Donovan closed the door.

"How do you *know* I didn't use the optical viewer?"

"I know. I heard your footsteps and there wasn't time. Lock that, will you?"

He stared at her a moment, then realized she was right. He hadn't locked his door, and if she hadn't mentioned it, he might not have realized it until he went to bed, when he made a point to routinely check locks.

Her intelligent gaze swept the penthouse again. "One of the first things I do is get a feel for the boundaries with new clients. Some people like their privacy and don't want me to disturb their things, or they want me to stay out of certain rooms. Other people want me anywhere and everywhere, attached to their hip so to speak. What about you, Dr. Knight? Any preferences? Any limits?"

He considered it. Attached at the hip sounded kind of interesting, though he could imagine some other places on her body where he might prefer to be attached.

''No, not really. Go ahead and snoop around, especially if you think it will help you do your job. You can go through my underwear drawer if it turns your crank.''

She glared at him, stone-sober. No giggles. No leaping on an opportunity.

This was new territory for sure.

''The guest room is down here,'' he told her, leading the way down the hall, fully aware that she knew exactly where it was. ''You know, I've never done this before and I'm not sure how to treat you. Like a guest, or an employee.''

''I'm neither. Mostly, treat me like I'm invisible. I'll take care of myself and try to stay out of your way as much as possible. We'll go over the contract tomorrow, and I can fill you in more on how I work. But it's late now, so...''

Donovan reached the door of the guest bedroom and held out his hand for her to enter first. As her tiny body brushed by his in the doorway, he breathed in the scent of her hair again. It smelled fruity, and the fragrance wafted by him and disappeared all too quickly, leaving him feeling a little parched, so to speak.

She glanced at the bottle of beer in his hand. ''What happened to the red wine in the fancy crystal glass?''

''My mood changed. You want one?''

She moved all the way into the room and set her bag on the bed. ''No, I never drink on duty. You like Canadian beer?''

He looked down at the label. God, she was observant. ''Yeah.''

''Me, too. I didn't take you for a beer drinker,

though.'' She unzipped her bag, pulled out a baby monitor and an alarm clock, which she set on the bedside table.

''That's two things then,'' he said.

''I beg your pardon?''

''Two things that have surprised you about me. Triathlons and beer.''

She smiled noncommittally. ''Yeah. Two things.'' She pulled out a laptop and set it on the bed, then unraveled the cord and went looking for an outlet.

Donovan continued to stand in the doorway. ''Can I get you anything? Towels? Something to eat? If you don't want a beer, there's orange juice and Perrier and Coke and...I think there's ginger ale—''

''I'm fine. If I want anything, I'll help myself if that's okay.''

''Sure.'' He continued to stand there while she plugged in her computer at the desk.

After a moment, she approached him. ''Look, you don't have to baby-sit me. It's my job to baby-sit *you*. I don't sleep much, so I'll be working late on some proposals for improvements to your alarm system, and making sure your place isn't bugged. I've got keen ears, and when I do sleep, I generally do it with one eye open, so you can relax and get a good night's sleep tonight, and not worry so much about being able to reach that baseball bat you've got stowed under your bed.''

Donovan slowly blinked. She'd noticed the bat, too. And she wanted him out of her hair. He couldn't remember the last time a woman had told him to go away, and certainly not in a bedroom doorway at this time of the night.

He never imagined rejection could feel so damn good. And so damn frustrating.

Sometime after three in the morning, wearing her tank top and plaid pajama bottoms, Jocelyn e-mailed her assistant, Tess. She gave her instructions to contact the two alarm system companies she trusted for quotes, and to arrange for Dr. Knight's locks to be changed first thing in the morning. She then shut off her computer and rubbed her burning eyes with the heels of her hands.

Dr. Knight seemed to prefer lamps that gave off dim, golden lighting. Relaxing and romantic, yes, but not very practical. She should have had the overhead light on, rather than staring at that bright screen in the semidarkness.

She rose from her chair to take her empty water glass back to the kitchen. After rinsing it out in the spotless, gleaming sink, she still didn't feel much like going to sleep, so she decided to look around the penthouse a bit more. She wandered leisurely around the kitchen.

Dr. Knight certainly had an impressive collection of cookbooks. He had an entire floor-to-ceiling bookcase full of them, and they covered everything from vegetarian cooking to Indian food to chocolate and poultry. Did he like to cook for himself? she wondered, imagining those hands of his stirring chocolate batter, cracking a delicate egg.

She could imagine those hands doing a lot of things—unbuttoning buttons, unzipping zippers, sliding beneath a waistband....

Something inside her tingled pleasurably as her mind meandered around that idea, but when she caught herself veering off the path of professionalism again, she shut her eyes and shook her head. She spent the next few minutes forcing herself to think about the penthouse, instead of the man who inhabited it.

Jocelyn made her way out into the main hall and walked slowly in her bare feet, checking out the paintings on the walls. Most of them were contemporary landscapes, with plenty of seascapes as well. Closer to the front door, there were more framed black-and-white photographs of old abandoned, dilapidated farm houses.

She peeked into Dr. Knight's exercise room and flicked on the light. He had a treadmill, a life cycle and a weight bench, and again, everything was shiny and clean. There wasn't a hint of clutter anywhere. She wondered how anyone could be so perfect all the time.

Where did he keep his junk? Did he even have any?

She crossed the room to check the window latches, even though she had already checked them a couple of hours ago, then realized with some uneasiness that she was overcompensating for something: a personal rather than professional interest in poking around. She had questions about the man down the hall, sleeping soundly in his bed for what must be the first time in days.

An image of Dr. Knight stretched out on that huge bed, his muscular arms and legs sprawled out, his sun-bronzed body tangled in that thick, down duvet, burned suddenly in her brain. Her vision had him sleeping in jockeys, but perhaps he slept in boxers. Or maybe nothing at all.

Damn, she was doing it again. She willed herself to stop, and tried to remember her rule about not permitting herself to entertain any *personal* curiosities about her clients.

Not to mention the fact that Dr. Knight seemed like Tom in every way, and she had no business feeling curious about anyone who resembled her ex—people who derived their joy from living in lavish penthouses, wearing expensive tuxes and being spotted at the opera.

Then again, a few little things had made her wonder if there was more to Dr. Knight than what appeared on the surface. The beer thing had thrown her.

She came to the telephone near the front door, and noticed the high-tech answering machine beside it. Since he'd told her she could go through his underwear drawer if she wanted to, she decided to listen to his messages. One never knew where clues about stalkers could emerge.

She pressed play and reached for the volume control so she could keep the messages from waking her client. The machine clicked as it kicked in.

"Hi, Donovan, it's Eleanor. I had a great time last week. Just wondering how you're doing. Give me a call." *Beep.*

"Donovan, where were you the other night? I missed you, baby. Oh, it's Christine." *Beep.*

"Hi, gorgeous. Where've you been? Call me when you get a chance. I have tickets to *Die Tageszeiten* on Saturday night, and no one to go with." *Beep.*

There was one message from Mark, then four more like the first—more women sounding desperate and needy, wondering why Donovan hadn't returned their calls.

Pitying those poor women, Jocelyn shook her head and slid back into security specialist mode. She returned to her computer to note the names of the women, and decided to ask Dr. Knight about them in the morning.

At 4:45 a.m., the baby monitor that Jocelyn had positioned by the front door woke her instantly. She heard the sound of a key in the lock. She sat up and grabbed her gun.

Slipping out of bed without making a sound, she glided out of the room and made her way down the hall. A woman was sneaking in, quietly closing the door while she made an effort to be quiet. Before she had a chance to turn around, Jocelyn was behind her with the gun pointed at her head. "Hold it!"

The woman screamed and jumped.

"Put your hands on your head!" Jocelyn ordered.

Dr. Knight's bedroom door flew open and he came hurling out. Jocelyn kept her eyes on the intruder. "Get back in your room, Dr. Knight."

"No, no, it's okay!" he said. "This is my housekeeper!"

Only then did Jocelyn feel her own heart racing and the searing sensation of adrenaline coursing through her veins. She lowered her weapon. "I thought you said she came in the morning! It's 4:45 a.m."

"She likes to start early."

Jocelyn's shoulders went slack. "You could've told me! What was I supposed to think when someone sneaks into your penthouse at this hour?"

Dr. Knight moved toward the woman at the door. "I do apologize, Mrs. Meinhard. I'm so sorry. This is Jocelyn Mackenzie. She's a security specialist. I hired her last night. Jocelyn, this is Brunhilde Meinhard.''

Shakily, the older woman turned around. Her gray hair was pulled into a tight bun on top of her head. Her glasses were large with clear, plastic rims—the old-fashioned kind from the eighties.

Jocelyn, feeling guilty for frightening the poor woman, held out her hand and gave her an apologetic smile. ''Hi.''

With trembling fingers and a limp, fishlike grip, Mrs. Meinhard shook Jocelyn's hand.

Suddenly uncomfortable in her skintight tank top and pajama bottoms, Jocelyn nodded politely and pointed toward her bedroom. ''Well, now that I'm up, I'll go get dressed.''

Neither Dr. Knight nor Mrs. Meinhard said a word. Jocelyn turned away from them.

In her bare feet, she padded down the hall, and to her chagrin, all she could think about was one thing: Her client wore pajama bottoms to bed. And Lord, what a chest.

She was in deep trouble.

Three

An hour later, showered and dressed, Jocelyn walked out of her room with her gun holstered under her arm, her blazer buttoned over it. She went to the kitchen to make a pot of coffee, and met Mrs. Meinhard who had already taken care of that and was now polishing the brass knobs on the white cabinetry.

"Good morning, again," Jocelyn said.

Mrs. Meinhard regarded her coolly. "Morning."

Jocelyn poured herself a cup of coffee and watched the housekeeper scrub the hardware. "Look, I'm sorry for what happened earlier. I didn't mean to frighten you, but Dr. Knight hired me to do a job, and that's what I was doing."

Saying nothing, the woman continued to scrub.

"I guess you weren't here when the attack happened," Jocelyn continued, taking a sip of coffee, "but is there anything you noticed that was out of place when you came in the next morning? Anything out of the ordinary that you might not have told the police?''

The woman straightened and folded her cloth. She spoke with a thick, German accent. ''I tell police everything.''

''I don't doubt that, ma'am, I'm just asking if there might be something you didn't think of before.''

''No. There is nothing. You work for police?''

Jocelyn carefully studied the woman's face. ''No, I'm a private Executive Protection Professional. E.P.P. for short.''

Mrs. Meinhard nodded, but Jocelyn suspected she wasn't completely sure what that meant.

Jocelyn fired out some more questions. ''Can you tell me anything about the people who visit Dr. Knight? What about friends or family? Do any of them have keys?''

She shook her head. ''Dr. Knight has no family— at least, none that come here.''

''No brothers or sisters?''

''I don't know.''

Jocelyn cleared her throat. How could a house-keeper, who worked in someone's home everyday for four years, not know if her employer had brothers or sisters? Then again, besides one framed picture of a young couple and a baby, there were no photographs of people anywhere, only landscapes and seascapes and old farm houses. Maybe Dr. Knight was at work most of the time when Mrs. Meinhard was here, and she was gone home when he entertained.

Still, it was strange.

''What about friends? Does his partner, Dr.

Reeves, have a key? Or what about any girlfriends, past or present?''

Again, she shook her head. ''No women. He goes out a lot, but there is no one.''

Jocelyn heard Dr. Knight's bedroom door open, and the sound of footsteps approaching. She expected to see him in his work clothes, but instead, he wore a tank and shorts.

Jocelyn felt a sharp tingling of awareness move through her. He looked nothing like he did last night in the tuxedo. In sneakers and a shirt that showed off his broad, muscular shoulders, he looked almost like a regular, everyday guy. Well, not too regular. Not with *that* body.

He passed through the kitchen, apparently on his way to the door. ''Morning.''

Jocelyn set down her cup and followed him. ''Wait a second, we were supposed to go over the contract this morning. Where are you going?''

''For a run.'' He reached the marble foyer and pulled open a small cabinet drawer to retrieve a key in a shoe wallet and fasten it to his sneaker.

''Not without me you're not. Did you forget what you hired me for? I'm not here to guard your penthouse. I'm here to guard *you*.''

He stared at her for a long moment. ''I was wondering how this was going to work.... Do you think you can keep up?''

She gave him a you've-got-to-be-kidding look.

''Of course you can. Sorry.'' He glanced down at her loafers. ''Even with those?''

She glanced down, too. ''Yes, with these, but I'd rather not risk an injury. Wait here and I'll change.''

"You have running gear?" His voice gave away his surprise.

She flipped her hair over her shoulder as she headed to her room. "I have everything. We can discuss the contract while we run."

Jocelyn placed the flat of her hands on the marble, vestibule wall, and leaned in for a calf stretch. She wore black, thigh-length Lycra shorts and a matching Y-back bra top. Her arms, shoulders and stomach were firmly toned, and just as Donovan had imagined last night as he'd watched her flicking window latches in that brown suit, she had a terrific, tight butt and long, suntanned legs to die for.

"Is there anything you *don't* do?" he asked.

She finished the stretch and bent into another one. "Cook."

"No? I love to cook."

"We'll get along well, then. You love to cook, and I love to eat what other people put in front of me."

Her delivery was deadpan, but there was something there that suggested again that she did have a sense of humor, even if she wasn't obvious about it.

Donovan suspected there was a lot more to his bodyguard than what she showed the world. No one could be as indifferent as she seemed to be, every day of their life. This had to be her professional persona, and he found himself wondering quite acutely what she was like around her closest friends. He'd give anything to see her smile or laugh. Maybe he should make that his goal for the day.

Donovan continued to watch her. "Anything else you don't know how to do?"

She pulled her arm across her chest to stretch her triceps. "I don't know how to fix cars. It's on my to-do list."

"Me, neither, but I can't say it's on mine."

"No, you probably hire people to do that kind of menial work."

Donovan grabbed onto his sneaker and lifted his foot for a thigh stretch. "Now, why do you say it like that? Like I'm a snob or something."

"I never said that."

"No, but you implied it with your tone, and it's not the first time."

She said nothing. She just continued to stretch.

"You're not much of a talker, are you?"

"Like I said, I try to be invisible."

"Invisible is one thing. Rude is another."

"I wasn't being rude."

"Yes, you were. I asked you a question, and you ignored me."

She glanced at him only briefly. "I didn't ignore you. I just didn't reply to what wasn't a question in the first place. It was an observation on your part, and you're entitled to your opinions."

Donovan stretched his hamstrings. "My opinions... God, I don't even remember what I said now. Do you always have this effect on men?"

Jocelyn ignored the last part of his question. She finished stretching and pressed the elevator button. "You said I implied you were a snob."

He snickered at her deadpan tone again, as he gazed down at her dainty profile. She was looking up at the lighted numbers over the elevator doors.

"So, did you?" he asked.

"Did I what?"

"Imply that I was a snob? You can't argue that *that* wasn't a question."

The elevator dinged, the brass doors opened and Jocelyn stepped inside. She held him back from entering, looked up at the ceiling, then motioned for him to follow. "If I implied it, I apologize. It's none of my business what kind of person you are."

Donovan pressed the lobby button. "So you don't deny it. You think I'm a snob."

Her mouth curved up in a half smile as she shook her head at him. It was a cute smile. A little on the devilish side, but cute. He'd like to see another one. A looser one. The kind of smile she'd have right after sex.

If she ever had sex. He imagined there'd be a few "walls of inhibition" that would have to come down first. Or be scaled.

He would enjoy that—scaling her walls.

"What does it matter what I think, Dr. Knight? I'm just your bodyguard."

"It matters a great deal. We're going to be in close quarters over the next little while, and call me vain, but I can't stand the idea of a woman not liking me, especially when she doesn't even know me. And why can't you call me Donovan?"

"Because our relationship is a professional one, and keeping those lines firmly drawn is important in my line of work, especially when I'm required to inhabit people's homes."

He nodded. "Ah, that makes sense. You could have said so last night, when the subject came up."

"I hadn't decided whether or not I was going to take the job last night."

The elevator reached the bottom floor, and they

crossed the lobby and passed through the large revolving doors. Once out on the street, they began to
jog alongside each other.

"How'd you get the scar on your left shoulder?"
she asked, never taking her eyes off what was ahead
of her.

"You don't miss a thing, do you? I was in a car
accident a year ago."

"Your fault?"

"No, I was rammed by another driver who ran a
red light. My door caved inward and broke my arm
and a few ribs. The glass cut me up pretty bad, but
it was all fixable. It took me a while to get back in
shape, though. I used to compete in triathlons, but
now I'm just in training."

"You seem like an exercise nut."

"I just like staying healthy."

They jogged a block or two, then Jocelyn said,
"Let's talk about the contract now, and what level
of protection you want from me."

Donovan settled into a comfortable pace, his
breathing controlled. "Since you're going to be in
my house anyway, we might as well go for the highest level."

"It'll cost you."

"Not a problem."

They jogged down to the lights and crossed the
street.

"First," she said, "let's start with your penthouse.
Do you want me to arrange every improvement possible? Or stick with just the alarm system? Either
way, I'll need to see your deed to ascertain if there
are any conditions of occupancy that might limit
what we do."

"I'll get you the deed right away, and if we can, let's go the whole nine yards. The only thing I ask is that you keep the improvements from standing out too much. I don't want my home to look like Fort Knox."

"That can be arranged. I already put together some ideas last night with that in mind, since I figured cosmetics would be important to you."

Donovan swerved around a spilled ice-cream cone on the sidewalk. "There you go again."

"What do you mean, 'there I go again'?" Her voice got a little haughty, and Donovan couldn't deny that he liked it. She was inching off that rock of indifference.

"The way you figured cosmetics would be important to me. Now you're implying that I'm shallow."

She laughed out loud, and it was everything he had hoped it would be—throaty, from the heart and unbelievably sexy. "I implied no such thing!"

They crossed the street and headed toward Lincoln Park, their running shoes tapping the ground in perfect unison. Donovan had to admit he enjoyed needling her to open up a little, and he wasn't sure why. He never felt the urge to prod the women he usually dated and get to know more about what they were like deep down. It was usually the other way around.

She was quiet for a moment. "Can we get back to the contract now?"

They jogged onto the running track in the park, and passed other runners along the way. "Sure. You were talking about the penthouse."

"Yes. I'll act as your contractor, hiring the appropriate experts to install a new alarm system, as well as to come in and make your doors and windows more secure. As far as personal protection, I'll accompany you everywhere for a daily fee, which will be payable every thirty days.''

"Even to work?''

"You said you wanted the highest level of protection.''

"I do, but I'm a heart surgeon. You'll have to sit in the waiting room all day. You won't find that tiresome?''

"It's my job, Dr. Knight.''

"What about days off? Surely you'll need holidays.''

"I take holidays between jobs.''

"What if you get sick?''

"I have colleagues I trust with my life, and we spell each other off in emergencies like that.''

Donovan felt sweat cooling his back between his shoulder blades. Jocelyn had a healthy glow on her face, too, but she wasn't working too hard, not by a long shot. She was clearly in great shape. "I thought you worked alone.''

"I do, but I didn't always.''

"These colleagues…buddies from the Secret Service?''

"You got it. There are a number of us who work privately now. We contract each other out whenever we require team details.''

They jogged in silence along the water, in perfect sync with each other, enjoying the fresh, early morning air. For a long time neither of them said anything, until they came to the end of the park.

"Ready to turn back?'' Jocelyn asked.

"Yeah, I usually go that way.'' He pointed.

She stopped and bent forward, her hands on her

knees as she tried to talk through deep breaths. "Really? We should go a different way then, and run somewhere else tomorrow."

He understood what she was getting at—it was a security thing—and nodded in the other direction. "That way through the park'll take a little longer, but we'll end up back where we started."

"Great." They began to run again, both of them covered in a shiny film of perspiration, but still keeping perfect pace. When they arrived back on Donovan's street, they walked for a bit to cool down before going inside. They passed by the security guard, who politely waved.

Jocelyn got on the elevator first, and like before, checked the ceiling before letting him get on.

"What are you checking for?" he asked, as he stepped inside.

"If the hatch is ajar, there could be someone up there."

On the way up to his penthouse, Donovan was intensely aware of the silence between them, and had to stop himself from gazing down at her just for the sheer pleasure of it.

God, she smelled good. Like the outdoors and fresh, clean sweat. What he wouldn't give to touch her now. To rub his fingers along her slick, bare shoulder.

His blood began to pulse in his veins, and for the first time in years, he felt nervous around a woman.

"Maybe on the way to your office this morning," she said, "we could talk about suspects."

He tried to imagine that. "We could, if you don't mind people listening in."

"What do you mean? What people?"

"The people on the El."

The doors opened, and he stepped off, but Jocelyn stayed on the elevator. Donovan had to put his arm in front of the door to keep it from closing while she was still inside.

"You take the train to your office?" she asked, sounding more than a little shocked.

Donovan couldn't help smiling, and this time, she smiled back.

"I'm doing it again, aren't I?" she asked.

"Yes, you are. I suppose you expected me to drive a Jag? Or maybe have a limo and driver?"

At last she stepped off the elevator and held her hands up in mock surrender. "Okay, I'm guilty this time."

Donovan paused in the vestibule. "Why do you have those impressions of me, anyway? Is it because I was wearing a tux last night? Do you think my life is one big cocktail party?"

She shrugged. "Something like that. You have to admit, though, appearances haven't exactly made you out to be Blue Collar Joe."

Laughing quietly, Donovan bent down to get his key out of his shoe wallet, then straightened. "I'm a pretty normal guy, you know."

"Sure. A normal guy who has the best of everything in one of the most expensive penthouses in downtown Chicago."

"You're very observant, I'll give you that, but what you see is not always all that's there. You can't possibly know what's going on *inside* a person, by seeing what kind of beer they drink or what kind of house they live in."

She rubbed her perspiring forehead. "Appearances

speak volumes about a person. Already I know that you like things to be perfect in your physical life, and you lack depth in the relationships in your personal life.''

Donovan felt his hackles rise. "Lack depth? God, it's one insult after another! Why would you think that about me?''

"Because I see how perfect everything is in your penthouse, and clearly with all the exercise and working out you do, the perfection of your *physical* appearance is very important to you. You don't have any close friends or family who visit you, and you have seven women on your answering machine, all waiting to be called back.''

He brow furrowed. "You listened to my messages?''

"You said I could go through your underwear drawer if I wanted. I didn't think your messages were too far a stretch, and I was looking for clues about possible stalkers.''

"And you think you found them.''

She shrugged again. "Disgruntled ex-lovers are classic suspects.''

Donovan inserted the key into the lock but didn't open the door. There was a lot he could tell her about his personal life to correct her on her impressions, but the last thing he wanted to do right now, while he was boiling mad, was become defensive and pour his soul out on the floor at her feet. Instead, he turned the tables on her.

"You think you've got me figured out, but what I want to know is, who are *you* to judge *me,* when you are clearly hiding inside a tough, cold exterior that shouts to the world to keep out? Answer that, Ms.

Mackenzie, and I promise I won't ask you any more personal questions for the duration of our professional relationship.''

He took some pleasure when he saw that he'd knocked her composure off-kilter. Her full lips were parted in astonishment, as if she had no idea what to say.

Then he added with a bite, ''That is, *if* this relationship lasts beyond a day. Cuz I sure as hell didn't intend to hire a bodyguard who thinks she's a therapist.''

Four

Hiding behind a tough, cold exterior that shouts to the world to keep out? Was that how he saw her?

For a few uncomfortable seconds, Jocelyn reflected upon his assessment of her. God, when had she turned into such a cold fish? Had she been alone too long and forgotten how to connect with people? Or was she dispassionate because she'd been dragged through the dirt by the people she'd allowed herself to trust in her life?

Her heart stung suddenly with a memory of being about five, climbing onto her father's lap for a hug, and being shoved off and yelled at because her fingers had been sticky.

Was that why she'd stopped trying to be close to people? Because of all the times like those in her childhood?

Jocelyn gazed up at Donovan, then consciously

swept away any concerns about her personality or demeanor, for it was not in her nature to feel sorry for herself, nor was this the time to be reflecting on her less than perfect childhood.

And hey, it was her job to be tough and cold!

She would have liked to tell him that, but she decided it would be completely unprofessional to enter into a debate with a client about the workings of her inner self. Best to just back down.

"I'm guilty again," Jocelyn said, holding her hands up in surrender as they stood outside his door. "I judged you, all right? I admit it. You're right, I don't know you very well and I'm sorry. Obviously there's more to you than I thought."

A great deal more, or you wouldn't be so interested in what's going on with me, her inner voice added.

"Now you're just trying to please your client."

"I'm sorry, all right?"

He looked taken aback. "You give in awfully easy for a tough bodyguard."

Jocelyn huffed. "It's my job to *prevent* showdowns, not engage the enemy unless absolutely necessary."

"And now you're calling me the enemy."

She shook her head. "No, I'm not."

"Well, I'm glad we got that clear."

They stood in the vestibule for a long time, staring at one another.

Jocelyn looked up at his finely chiseled cheekbones and smoldering green eyes, and felt her insides quiver with pleasantly erotic responses—responses she had no right feeling, especially when he had just tried to interrogate her about her personal life.

She wasn't used to questions like those. Clients never wanted to know about her situation. They always wanted to remain apart.

She was still shaken. Her belly was fluttering with nervous butterflies.

God, what was it about him that made her react like an adolescent schoolgirl when that's not how she wanted to react? What was it that made her forget who she was—an untouchable, invisible Executive Protection Professional—and want to melt like hot cream into his capable hands?

Obviously, he was well-practiced in the art of seduction. That's probably what those questions were about. He looked for a woman's weakness and leaped on it.

He blinked slowly at her. "You should give in more often, you know."

A sudden image of giving in to him *on his bed* burned in her brain. "I beg your pardon?"

Get a grip, Jocelyn. You're reacting to his masculine appeal and reading too much into everything he's saying. He isn't making a sexual reference.

"Your face…" He reached one hand up to touch the center of her forehead with his thumb. "All the tension right here. It's gone. You look…softer."

His thumb feathered along her eyebrow while his warm palm cupped her cheek, and her knees, damn them, turned to pudding. Who would have thought a man touching her eyebrow would have such a debilitating effect on her?

She didn't know what to say. The line had been crossed, and she wasn't used to being on this side of it—weak-kneed and foggy-brained with a client, after an inappropriate conversation about her character, a conversation that had left her contemplating the ramifications of her childhood.

She wet her lips and struggled to keep her breathing steady, struggled to keep herself from wondering what it would feel like to kiss those beautiful full lips of his.

"You can relax," he said, "I'm not going to fire you."

"I'm perfectly relaxed."

"Yeah? I don't think so." He gave her an amused grin that told her he was arrogantly aware of his ability to reduce women to happy blobs of jelly whenever he felt the urge.

Jocelyn tried to steel herself against his liquefying effect. "I'm not one of your girlfriends, you know."

"I never thought you were."

Why wasn't he lowering his hand? He was tickling her ear now, and goose bumps were shimmying their way down her entire left side.

"I mean," she said in her best tough-girl voice, reaching up to gently remove his hand from under her hair—and it was one of the hardest things she ever did—"you're my client and this isn't exactly appropriate conduct."

That look of amusement never left his eyes. His mouth lifted in a wicked, sexy grin. "I knew that was coming. Maybe I should fire you after all."

"And risk opening that door to your stalker?" she said in a deep throaty voice.

Something had taken over—the same flirtatious spark that had bucked when she'd made that remark in the elevator the night before, about going to get her jammies and toothbrush. Her voice had taken on that teasing tone again. Now *she* was sounding seductive!

Where was this coming from? This was nothing like her. She wasn't acting professionally; she was playing hard to get.

He glanced at the door with the key still in the lock, then back at her face. His gaze dropped to her lips.

She could see he was impressed by her ''apparent'' immunity to his charms. And tempted. He wanted to kiss her. For a heart-stopping moment, she thought he might, and she was glad in a triumphant sort of way that she was turning him to jelly, too.

She quickly reminded herself, however, not to get cocky, when she wasn't entirely sure she would be able to resist him if he did try to kiss her.

Thank God he backed off. He tilted his head as if he were disappointed she'd stood her ground. ''I guess not.''

He pushed the door open, but she wrapped her hand around his firmly muscled upper arm to stop him from going in first. It was damp with perspiration and the intimacy of touching his warm, wet skin at that moment—after what had just occurred between them—was painfully erotic. She felt the heat of the connection straight down to her toes.

Pushing those feelings down into the deepest reaches of her being, and summoning her acute, well-honed bodyguard senses, she went through the door first. ''Mrs. Meinhard? Are you here?''

''In the kitchen!'' she heard the woman call out.

''Is everything all right?''

''It's fine!''

Nevertheless, Jocelyn had Donovan wait inside by

the door while she checked out the penthouse. "It's all clear," she said when she returned.

But it wasn't all clear. Not by a long shot, because her heart was still pounding out a cacophony in her chest. All because of her client's blatant sexual appeal, his discerning ability to see through her tough-girl image and her own inability to keep her head on straight about it.

That night, after a long day in the hospital, Donovan changed into a pair of faded old blue jeans and a T-shirt, then sank into his plush, white sofa. He crossed one leg over the other on the glass and wrought iron coffee table. He had just ordered Chinese food, and Jocelyn had gone into her room for a few minutes to make sure the alarm system would be installed tomorrow as scheduled.

He stared at the dark windows, enjoying the silence for a moment, thinking about their conversation in the vestibule that morning.

When he'd gone up against all her judgmental observations with one of his own, he had completely disarmed her. She'd backed down quicker than a spooked rabbit.

What was her story? She didn't want him getting into her personal life, yet she was perfectly comfortable and eager to get into his.

She would probably argue that it was the nature of her job—to learn everything she could about the people she was sworn to protect—but he didn't buy that. When he'd asked her about *her* personal life, the shock and fear on her face had come from deep down inside. He'd seen panic in her eyes, as if no one had ever tried to reach in and pull out her soul before. It had been disturbing to her.

Why also, he wondered, did she have such strong negative opinions about his lifestyle? He wasn't a criminal, yet she looked upon him—and everything he owned—with disapproval and disdain.

He stood up, went to the CD player and inserted *Eric Clapton, Unplugged,* to try and clear his head. Sounds of a jazzy guitar filled the large room, and within seconds, Jocelyn came down the hall, still wearing her brown trousers and white blouse, though she'd unfastened the top few buttons. The blazer was gone, the part in her hair was crooked; her blouse was slightly untucked. To be honest, she looked a little bedraggled from the day.

She was completely adorable.

There was a different expression on her face tonight, one he hadn't seen before. It was…mellow.

She raised her eyebrows. "You listen to Eric Clapton?"

"All the time."

Jocelyn stood in the arched entry to the living room with her hand on one of the white columns, listening for a moment, then she began to move slowly, languidly into the room. Her voice was nostalgic and lighthearted when she spoke. "I haven't heard this in ages. I used to listen to it in my car. I drove to Florida once for a vacation, and played it over and over. It was great."

He smiled at her personal reminiscence and sat down. "When was that?"

"Oh, four years ago. I haven't had a vacation since."

"Sounds like you could use one."

"Not really. I like to work."

He sat down on the sofa again. She sat at the other end.

"Everybody needs time off."

"I get time off between assignments, although I'm usually doing the advance work for the next one. But you know what they say—a change is as good as a rest."

"Maybe." Just then, the doorbell chimed. "It's the food." Donovan stood to answer it, but Jocelyn stopped him.

"Let me." She went to the door and used the peephole, then opened it using the chain. "How much, please?"

The delivery man told her. "Just a minute." She closed the door again and locked it.

Donovan was right behind her with a couple of bills. "He can keep the change."

She opened the door and paid the man, then closed it and turned all the locks again.

"You are certainly thorough," he said, carrying the large paper bag toward the kitchen.

"It's what you pay me for."

She followed him into the kitchen. They pulled the white boxes out of the bag and set them on the large, marble-topped center island.

Jocelyn pulled out the wooden chopsticks.

"I have better ones here somewhere," Donovan said, pulling open drawers until he found his good set. He fetched plates, then sat next to Jocelyn on one of the stools.

They popped open a couple of cans of ginger ale, then served themselves and began to eat.

"You have a beautiful formal dining room, and I suppose you eat here most of the time."

"Yeah, I do. Everything's handy here, and it's just usually me anyway."

"But I thought you liked to cook." She poured her fizzing ginger ale into a glass. "I'd imagined you inviting dinner companions over, to impress them with your gourmet meals and fancy cutlery."

He drew his eyebrows together to give her a look that told her she was doing it again.

She covered her mouth with a hand. "God, I'm sorry."

He swallowed. "Apology accepted, on one condition."

"Uh-oh. I don't like the sound of that." Her playful tone sparked an awareness of her as a woman again. Damn his libido.

"Don't worry," he replied. "It's nothing indecent. Not that I wouldn't enjoy a little indecency with my very attractive bodyguard, but somehow I doubt it's in your job description."

She grew serious. "Even talking about it is inappropriate, Donovan."

Hearing her use his given name for the first time— after urging her unsuccessfully more than once in the past twenty-four hours—sent his pulse on a bumpy road trip.

"I understand that," he said soberly. "I don't mean to make your job difficult. I just can't help it every once in a while. You're a very attractive woman."

He saw her swallow hard. "And you're an attractive man, but we're both adults and more than capable of controlling our baser instincts, especially when there's danger involved. Someone might be trying to kill you, and I can't afford to lose my focus."

He nodded, feeling somewhat disappointed in her unwavering proclamation of "self-control." Feeling that way was completely ridiculous, he knew. He'd hired her to do a job and do it well, not act negligently and become his lover. He *wanted* her to be reliable. Didn't he?

Jocelyn sipped her ginger ale. "You still haven't told me the condition involved in your accepting my apology."

"Ah, yes. The condition." He wiped his mouth with a napkin. "Well, you've expressed these somewhat biased perceptions of me more than once, and I would like to know why you have them, or more importantly, why you seem to disapprove of me."

She inhaled deeply and moved her spring roll around on her plate with a chopstick. "I don't disapprove of you. I barely know you."

"You *do* disapprove of me, and you're also great at avoiding questions."

"And you're great at being bold."

"Still avoiding."

She gazed directly at him, incredulous. "You don't give up, do you?"

"Nope."

Eric Clapton's "Layla" started to play in the other room, its sexy rhythm lightening the tension-filled silence. Donovan watched Jocelyn lean against the wrought iron back of the bar stool. Her lips were glossy from the cherry sauce.

What he wouldn't give to taste the flavor of those sweet, sticky lips....

His body began to react tumultuously to the image of his mouth on hers, so he swerved his thoughts back around to what he and Jocelyn had been talking about a few seconds ago. He'd asked her a question and she hadn't answered it.

He waited.

And waited.

She poked a chicken ball and swirled it around in the red sauce. "All right, if you must know, I used to be involved with a doctor, years ago. Only he wasn't a doctor at the time. He was in medical school."

"What, the guy was a jerk, so all doctors are jerks? Or you're not over him, and I remind you of it?"

"No, it's neither of those things."

"What is it then?"

Lord, talking to her was like getting blood from a stone.

She took a drink. "We lived together when he was going through school, and I supported both of us while I put off going to the police academy. Then, as soon as he graduated, he dumped me and went off to marry a rich debutante, and basically changed his whole identity. He bought a Mercedes Benz, started going to the opera and ballet, when he was never into that sort of thing with me. We used to go to hockey games and sports pubs where the draft was cheap. I guess the worst part was that he'd been seeing this woman while he was still with me. He lied to me and left me with all the debt I'd incurred to support us while he was in school, and never looked back. I met him once a couple of years ago in a bookstore, and he was with his wife. He never even acknowledged me. They treated me like I was dirt under their shoes—in another class far below them.''

''So that's why you disapprove of me? You think that just because I own a penthouse and go to the opera occasionally, I'm a stuffed shirt?''

He hoped she realized how mistaken she was. He didn't grow up with this wealth. He had come into it later when he would have given anything to trade it for what he had lost. God, he'd trade all of it today and live like a pauper, if it would mean he could erase the tragedy from his childhood, and see and touch the parents he never really knew. Even just for an instant.

He swallowed over the aching sense of loss that still lived deep inside him—the fleeting, vague memories, like little fragments of a dream: his mother's loving smile, his father's boisterous laughter as he swung Donovan around in circles. If only he could remember more...

He brushed the grief aside, like he'd learned to do years and years ago, and brought himself back to the present.

''It's not just that.'' Jocelyn gestured around the room with a hand. ''Tom became a doctor to have this very thing. For the prestige. It had nothing to do with wanting to help people. This kind of lifestyle was more important to him than any person ever could be.''

''I see, and because I'm a successful doctor and live alone and have women leaving messages on my answering machine, I don't care about people, either?''

She shrugged.

"You really don't know much about me, Jocelyn. You realize that, don't you?"

Nodding, she seemed to agree. He was glad. Maybe he'd give her the whole story sometime.

"I said I was sorry before," she replied. "Old habits and values die hard, that's all."

Donovan gazed at her face while she fiddled with her food. She'd barely eaten half of what was on her plate.

"Look," he said, "I didn't mean to put you on the spot or make you feel bad or anything."

"I don't feel bad."

He lightened his tone, smiling. "Yes, you do."

Thank goodness she smiled, too. She picked up her fortune cookie, wrapped in plastic, and hurled it across the corner of the island to hit him in the chest. "I don't."

Donovan laughed. "Okay, okay." He looked at the cookie in his hand. "Is this yours or mine? I don't want to mess with fate and get the wrong fortune."

She picked up the other one. "It's yours. I want this one."

They both opened their packets. "What does yours say?" he asked.

"It says, 'You are a deep, complex individual.' What about yours?"

"Hmm. Let me see." He broke the cookie and unfurled the little piece of paper. "Wow. It says, 'You're going to get lucky tonight.' What do you think it means by that?"

Her face lit up like a baseball park at night. "Let me see that!" She grabbed it out of his hands. "It does not say that you big jerk! It says 'You like to fix things.'''

She handed it back to him, then rose to clean away the dishes and put the leftovers in the fridge. "Nice try though."

Donovan watched her from behind. Unfortunately, not nice enough.

Five

———

He was a brilliant heart surgeon, Jocelyn learned from just about everyone she talked to about Donovan at the hospital. The best around. Nice man, too, they all said, including the nurses, who didn't seem to imply that he ever tried to make moves on them, which was somewhat surprising to Jocelyn, considering how many moves he'd tried to make on her the past couple of days.

The thought sent a shiver dancing down her spine, as she sat in Donovan's waiting room reading a magazine and remembering all the times he'd given her ''that look.''

It was like he thought she was hot stuff....

Another shiver went down her spine, close on the trail of the first one.

She couldn't deny that she enjoyed those looks from him. It was flattering, especially because she'd never imagined herself as "hot." She wore plain suits and flat shoes to work, sensible cotton underwear. She had a conservative shoulder-length hair cut, and she was definitely *not* a flirt. In fact, she made a conscious effort *not* to give off signals—at least the kind that alerted hungry male hormones to a potential meal. She didn't spread her scent around. Consequently, she was dull. Downright dull.

In her defense, being dull came with the job. She didn't go places with her principals to be a part of their social lives. She wanted to blend in, to be polite and generally not speak unless spoken to, and where possible be invisible. In addition to that, she had to be paranoid all the time and keep an attitude that no one was to be trusted, which didn't exactly make her Miss Charisma at social functions.

Hence—she was dull.

Jocelyn lowered her magazine, feeling suddenly dissatisfied. Throughout her life, it seemed like she'd always made a conscious effort to be dull, whether it was in the way she dressed or the way she talked.

Why? Was it because she'd grown up being pushed to act cute in front of the neighbors and wear fancy dresses with lace, her hair in shiny curls? Was it because that was the only time anyone seemed to approve of her—when her appearance was perfect or noteworthy—and this was some sort of rebellion against that kind of shallow thinking?

She continued to flip through the fashion magazine, looking at all the skinny, glamorous models with big hair and small boobs. *Blah.* She didn't want to compare herself to them. She'd spent her whole life reminding herself that it was what was on the inside that mattered....

She shut the magazine and tossed it onto the table in front of her chair, thinking more about Donovan and the way he flirted with her.

How long had it been since she'd had a date with a man? she wondered. Ages. Sure, she went out with her professional colleagues for a beer occasionally, and they were mostly men, but those weren't dates. They all treated her like one of the guys.

It was the female signal thing.

She wouldn't know how to send one out if her life depended on it.

Not that it did.

Yet, Donovan was responding to something....

The door to his office opened, and a middle-aged woman walked out. Donovan, wearing a cotton shirt and jeans and sneakers beneath his lab coat, followed her out. She stopped at the reception desk to speak to the nurse, and was laughing at something Donovan was saying to her.

Carrying his clipboard, he turned away from her and said, "Enjoy yourself at the golf tournament, Marion."

He was certainly charming, and very caring with his patients. He seemed less and less like Tom every day. No wonder everyone liked him.

He passed through the waiting room and glanced down at Jocelyn—who sat in a chair like the other patients—and winked at her.

Heat licked all the way down to her toes and back up again. She forced herself to smile politely and open up another magazine, but God! He was so gorgeous! She couldn't breathe. She didn't have a clue what she was even looking at. Ads? Articles? Little green men?

Jocelyn cleared her throat and tried to calm her clanging heart, but she couldn't. She discreetly glanced around the quiet room, wondering if anyone else could hear it. Apparently not.

She watched Donovan invite the next patient in—an elderly gentleman with a walker.

"George, how are we doing today?" Donovan said to the man, just before he closed the door behind him.

Jocelyn continued to flip idly through her magazine, repeating to herself over and over in her head: He's your client, you idiot. Your client, your client, your client.

Contrary to Donovan's usual routine of taking the El to work and back, they started taking his car, as Jocelyn didn't feel it was safe to walk to the train at the same time each day, nor to stand in the crowded compartment, where anyone could pull a knife without warning and be gone just as fast.

In the parking lot after work, she conducted her usual vehicle search before allowing Donovan to get in. She began by checking the small pieces of tape she routinely affixed at inconspicuous spots along the door, hood and trunk openings, to detect if the vehicle had been tampered with during the day. Then she proceeded with a detailed search of the interior and exterior of the car, looking for trip wires, stripped screws, leaking fluids and such. Donovan waited nearby, watching.

She gave the vehicle a clean bill of health and got in. Donovan got behind the wheel and they headed home.

"How about dinner and the theater tonight?" he

asked her, shifting gears and gaining speed out on the road.

The question caught her off guard. Principals didn't usually ask her to dinner with them—not phrased like that anyway.

He gave her a perceptive, sidelong glance, taking his eyes off the road only for a brief second. "Sorry. What I should have said is, 'I'm going to eat out tonight and take in a play. I'll need you to work late.'"

Jocelyn smiled, appreciating his courteous rephrasing of the invitation. "Yes, sir."

"I'd like to go to an upscale place for dinner, so if you're going to fit in, you won't be able to wear that."

She glanced down at her suit. "Uh, I don't really have anything with me that's—"

"We'll get something for you on the way home." He turned down a street in the opposite direction from where he lived.

"Really, you don't have to buy me clothes," Jocelyn said. "We can stop by my apartment and I can pick something up."

"You live on the other side of town. This'll be much quicker. I know a great spot."

She reluctantly agreed, and they drove down a narrow, tree-lined street. Donovan pulled up in front of an exclusive ladies' boutique on the bottom floor of a late-Victorian mansion, and turned off the car. "What are you…a size five?"

"Seven, actually," she replied awkwardly.

"Great. Let's go."

He led the way in, and bells chimed over the door as they entered. An older lady with her hair in a bun, wearing a pale yellow silk suit and pearls, approached. "Dr. Knight, what a pleasure. What can I help you with today?"

They know him here?

"Actually, Doris, you can help my friend. We're going to La Perla tonight."

"Lovely." She turned her warm gaze on Jocelyn, who felt more than a little out of place in this high-end clothing shop. It was not a place she would ever set foot in on her own.

"I have some stunning gowns over here that would look wonderful on you," Doris said. She gestured for Jocelyn to follow. Donovan followed, too. Doris picked a gold, sequined dress off a brass rack. "What about this?"

Jocelyn glanced down at the tag. The dress cost nine hundred and fifty dollars. Good God. "Uh, that might be a little too…"

"Too flashy?" Doris said. "I understand. What about this?" The smiling woman moved to another rack and presented a deep crimson off-the-shoulder dress. It was twelve hundred dollars.

Jocelyn touched her index finger to her lips. "That, I think, is…um…"

"Not the right color?"

Not the right price! "Yes, exactly."

"Okay, I think I know exactly what you're looking for." Doris moved to the corner of the boutique and found a black, sleeveless, curve-hugging dress with a train. "Perfect for La Perla."

"Perfect for Jocelyn," Donovan said, moving past her and touching the delicate fabric.

Jocelyn didn't dare look at the price tag on that

one. The odd thing was, Donovan didn't look at it, either.

She shook her head in utter disbelief. *The rich.*

Feeling more than a little uncomfortable with all this, Jocelyn looped her arm through Donovan's and gently pulled him away from Doris. "Could I have a word with you?" she whispered politely.

"Sure." They moved behind a mannequin dressed in a sailing outfit.

"This is too much," Jocelyn whispered. "I can't let you buy me a dress here."

"Why not?" he asked innocently.

"Because it's too expensive. I couldn't possibly accept a gift like this."

"It's not *that* expensive. Not relatively."

"Relative to what?"

"To…to other shops. Really, twelve hundred's not that much for a dress like that."

"What, twelve *thousand* would be more in line with what you'd call expensive?"

"Well, yeah."

She felt the difference between them like a deep chasm at that moment. Twelve hundred dollars was pocket change to him.

"And how do you know about prices of dresses anyway?" she asked, still whispering. "And how does Doris know your name? Do you often come here to buy clothes for your lady friends? The ones who leave messages on your answering machine? The ones you never call back?"

He raised his eyebrows, looking amused. "You sound jealous."

"I am *not* jealous. I just find it odd that the clerk here knows you by name and—"

"What about this one?" Doris said, appearing un-expectedly behind Jocelyn, who felt her face color.

"I liked the other one better," Donovan said.

Doris went away, and he took a step closer to Joc-elyn to whisper in her ear. "Why don't you just try it on? I really want to see you in it."

His hot, moist breath sent goose bumps tingling down her body. Oh, where was her iron hormonal resistance mechanism when she needed it?

"Why?" she asked. "This isn't a date we're going on. I'm just there for your security. You don't need to dress me up in something I guarantee I'll never wear again."

"You said yourself that you need to blend in. This is appropriate for where we're going."

Jocelyn gazed at his imploring expression for a long time, then remembered one of the strict rules of her profession: *It's not my job* should never be thought or spoken.

It was her duty to always ensure that her principal felt secure and comfortable, whether that meant rais-ing an umbrella over his head if it started to rain, or making sure that his luggage didn't get lost on a flight across the country. In this case, if seeing her dressed to "fit in" with the clientele at the restaurant would make her principal feel more at ease, then she had to do as she was asked.

With a deep sigh of defeat, she raised her hands in the air. "All right, I'll try it on."

"Thank you," he whispered close to her ear, caus-ing another torrent of goose bumps to tickle all over her skin.

Doris led her into an enormous wallpapered change room with a small mahogany table and lamp inside, as well as a brocade settee. There were three pairs of patent leather shoes on a low shelf, for the customers to use.

Lord, this was not her life.

She tried on the floor-length gown, slipped the heels on her feet, then turned to look at herself in the mirror.

Good God. Her heart almost skipped a beat. It had to be someone else's reflection she was looking at. The dress hugged all her curves—curves she wasn't even aware she possessed—and made her look so-phisticated and radiant, like a movie star on the red carpet. *Like a woman.*

A knock sounded at the dressing room door. "How are you doing?" Doris asked. "Can I get you anything?"

Feeling uncertain and turning around carefully—for she wasn't used to walking in high-heeled shoes—Jocelyn slowly grasped the crystal knob and stepped out. She tried to ignore how uncomfortable and ridiculous she felt.

Doris smiled and nodded. "That's the one."

Jocelyn, who had kept her head down since she'd opened the door, finally looked up. Donovan's lazy gaze was moving slowly up and down the length of her body.

Her heart held still, waiting for what he would say, while she chided herself for letting it matter. She shouldn't care what she looked like in his eyes. In fact, she should hate the fact that he wanted to dress her up like her father used to do. She wasn't a doll or an ornament.

Yet, another part of her felt oddly liberated seeing herself this way. All through her life she had resisted

her natural urges to wear something pretty, to feel
soft and feminine, because she didn't want to be valued for that. She wanted to be valued for something
deeper.

Contemplatively, Donovan tilted his head to the
side and stared into her eyes. "Yes, this is definitely
the one."

The restaurant was small, intimate and very romantic.

Located in the low-ceilinged basement of an old
stone mansion in a quiet part of town, it was dimly
lit with flickering candles and staffed with soft-
spoken waiters in tuxedos. White-clothed tables—set
with sparkling crystal wineglasses and shiny silver
utensils—were spaced apart in little alcoves or sur-
rounded by creeping ivy plants to provide privacy. It
was the perfect place for a discreet affair.

Jocelyn had called ahead to arrange for cooperation regarding Donovan's security, and had ascer-
tained that this would be a low-risk detail, judging
by the floor plan the manager had faxed over to her.
Still, she kept her gun strapped to her ankle and
looked around the restaurant with discerning eyes as
they were led to their table in the back corner.

"So this is where the theater crowd comes?" Jocelyn commented, sitting down while Donovan stood
behind her and slid her chair forward.

He took the seat across from her. Behind him, a
trellis of greenery closed him in; the gray stone wall
provided enclosure. The waiter poured water for
them and Donovan ordered wine.

"So you never told me how you know Doris,"

Jocelyn said, making conversation after the waiter disappeared.

Donovan's lips curved up in a slow-burning smile. "Have you been carrying that question around all afternoon and evening?"

"Really, I haven't given it a thought until now."

He gave her an exaggerated, knowing nod that told her he was completely aware that she had been curious since they'd left the shop, and was amused by it.

How was it possible a man could be so arrogantly sure of himself regarding her thoughts and feelings?

"If you must know, Doris was a patient of mine," he said.

Oh.

Jocelyn continued to gaze at him, realizing she'd jumped to conclusions again, and deciding that tonight, she was going to at long last figure this man out, and prove or disprove every first and last mistaken impression she had of him.

"I can't tell you more than that," he continued, "because of doctor-patient confidentiality, only that I trust her good taste."

"I see. I thought…"

He was amused again; the playful tone in his voice revealed it. "I know what you thought—that I take all my lovers there to dress them up to my liking, or impress them and buy favors."

Jocelyn shook her head at herself and grinned apologetically. This was ridiculous. She had to get her act together.

"Donovan," she said point-blank. "If we're going to have any kind of normal working relationship, it's time I did some intelligence gathering."

"Intelligence gathering? Jocelyn, you're a riot. How about we just have a conversation, like two normal people out to dinner together, getting to know each other?"

She nervously cleared her throat. Where were her social skills when she needed them? She supposed—on top of her glamorous attire this evening—she wasn't used to clients taking her out to quiet, romantic restaurants for dinner. Usually, she, in her flat brown shoes and starchy white shirt, sat at a nearby table alone while her clients had dinner with *other* people.

But apparently, Donovan wanted this to be like a date, and she had no idea how to behave with a rich, handsome doctor who knew which fork to use and how to order the wine.

Add to that the complexity of her trying to behave professionally and *not* be charming—as if she would know how—for she didn't want this to be too enjoyable for either one of them. That could lead to dangerous places.

"All right," she said nonetheless. "Let's get to know each other. How about we start with the messages on your answering machine? How is it possible that you could be seeing seven women at the same time? Do they know about each other?"

She made sure she kept her tone light and friendly, so she wouldn't come off sounding like a jealous, judgmental shrew.

He leaned back in his chair. "I'm not really *seeing* any of them. We're all mostly just friends."

"Mostly."

He wet his lips. "I'm thirty-four years old, Jocelyn. I'm not a monk."

If this wasn't such a high-class joint and she wasn't wearing these strappy heels, she would have crawled under the table and cringed, and stayed there until after dessert was served. "Of course, I didn't mean to imply…"

"It's okay. That's what we're doing tonight, isn't it? Cutting to the chase? While we're on the topic of those women, I might as well tell you that I'm not involved with any of them now. I've been busy lately and keeping to myself. I haven't had much of a social life, and contrary to what you think, those messages you heard didn't all come the day you arrived. They've been accumulating over the past couple of months, and I've been saving them only because I never seem to get around to returning the calls."

"But what if they've all been sitting by the phone all this time, waiting for you to call?"

"I doubt any of them have been sitting by their phones, at least not over me. They'd move on to the next guy pretty quickly."

"How can you be so sure? Maybe one or two of them truly are waiting for you to call. Maybe you're treating them carelessly and you don't realize it."

"No, Jocelyn, I wouldn't do that." His voice was so direct, his tone so indisputable, she couldn't even contemplate not believing him. "Besides, none of them ever had their hearts invested in me. It was only their ambitions."

"Their ambitions?"

"Yes. You know, the Won't-Mother-be-proud-if-I-snag-myself-a-rich-doctor kind of ambitions."

"How do you know?"

"I *just know*. And I never wanted that kind of a

superficial relationship, no matter how attractive or successful a woman was.''

She gazed into his smoldering, green eyes, stunned by everything he was saying. She knew she had been misjudging him all this time, but she'd had no idea to what extreme. She'd imagined he was the kind of man who would use other people for his own enjoyment, but in fact, it seemed to be the other way around. He was the one being used, and he—as far as she could see—didn't like it.

Shallow, he was not.

"Is that why you've never married?"

"Yes and no. I haven't met the right woman, certainly, but I haven't really been looking, either. Marriage just isn't at the top of my to-do list these days."

"So what's been keeping you so busy lately?" she asked, changing the subject. "Besides watching out for stalkers?"

"I've been raising funds for a grief counseling center for children."

"No kidding." The waiter brought the wine and Donovan tasted it and gave it the proverbial thumbs-up. The waiter began to pour some in Jocelyn's glass, but she stopped him after the first splash. "That's enough, thank you." She never drank on the job.

"Are you ever going to let your hair down around me?"

"My hair is down."

"You know what I mean. Are you ever going to forget that you're my bodyguard, and just be a woman?"

Jocelyn cleared her throat. The implications of that question were disturbing to say the least, especially the way she'd been feeling lately.

"That might be dangerous. If I let down my guard, even for a minute, that would be the time something disastrous would happen. Rule of the trade."

That wasn't the only reason why it would be disastrous, but she didn't want to go there.

Donovan sat across from Jocelyn, admiring the way she looked in the flickering candlelight, wearing that elegant off-the-shoulder black dress with the earrings Doris had helped her pick out to match.

He could tell by the way Jocelyn carried herself that she had absolutely no idea—not a clue—how incredibly beautiful she was.

Or how she was driving him insane keeping him on this side of the table, with the bodyguard-principal lines so firmly drawn. He'd chosen this restaurant for a reason, so she could relax for a few hours between walking in and walking out, and he could have a chance to try and bring out the woman in her.

Because he knew there was a real woman in there—a fascinating and passionate one—buried somewhere deep down inside and anxious to come out. He could see it in her dark, mysterious, dazzling eyes.

He wasn't imagining that there was something between them, either—something she was fighting with all her might.

The waiter returned and took their orders, then made a slight bow and departed.

"So why have *you* never married?" Donovan asked before taking a long sip of wine. He noticed she didn't touch hers.

She leaned forward, put her elbow on the table and rested her chin on her hand. "I don't really believe in happily ever after, and I prefer being on my own."

"Do you really?"

"Yes, I really do."

"What about your parents? Where are they?"

"My mother died six years ago, and my father is somewhere in the Midwest."

"You don't know where he lives?"

"No, my parents divorced when I was fourteen, and he never kept in touch. It was best that way. It would have been too hard on my mother to see him. He broke her heart when he left her for a younger woman."

Donovan reached across the table and touched her warm, slender hand. "I'm sorry to hear that. She never remarried?"

"No, and I can't blame her. After what Dad did, it would've been pretty hard to trust anyone again."

This tough, untouchable bodyguard was becoming more clear to Donovan by the minute. The only two men she'd ever been close to had both left her and never looked back. She was bound to be wary of relationships.

A few minutes later, their appetizers arrived, and they talked about other things. Jocelyn told him about her experiences in the Secret Service, as well as what it was like going through the police academy. Some of her stories were downright hilarious, and she had him in stitches with a few of her tales. There were some hair-raising incidents, too, when she'd come face-to-face with attackers and had to use her combat skills. Mostly, though, she described her job as being pretty quiet. Prevention was everything.

After dinner, they drove to the theater where they sat in Donovan's regular box seats, and Jocelyn seemed to enjoy the play immensely. When they finally arrived home it was almost midnight, and they rode up in the elevator, smiling and talking about the actors.

When they reached the top floor, Jocelyn removed her heels in the vestibule, disarmed the new, state-of-the-art alarm system inside, then searched the penthouse thoroughly. Once she'd ensured everything was normal, she returned to where Donovan waited near the door.

"Everything's fine. We can relax now."

"We can?" He tried not to think of all the ways he would like to relax with this incredible woman he had invited into his home. This beautiful, appealing, sexy woman who set his loins on fire.

"Since you put it like that, how about joining me for a nightcap?"

"You know I don't drink on the—"

"On the job, yeah I know, but we're home now and you've already searched the place. The new alarm system is up and running for later in the night. Surely you can consider yourself off duty for the next hour. Just one glass of wine. Or pop. Your choice."

Jocelyn sighed heavily. "I haven't had a glass of wine in eons."

He spread his hands wide. "I have just about every kind you can imagine—Shiraz, merlot, sauvignon blanc, Chardonnay—you name it."

"Well, I did want to talk to you some more about who could be stalking you."

"We can talk about whatever you want."

She hesitated for a few seconds. "I guess one glass of merlot wouldn't hurt."

"Excellent." He backed away from her toward the

kitchen. "Don't go away. I'll bring it to you. Just make yourself comfortable."

Donovan left Jocelyn in the living room and went to pour two glasses of the best red wine he had in his collection.

Six

Donovan brought the wine into the living room where Jocelyn sat, curled up on his huge white sofa.

He stopped in the entranceway. God, he couldn't get over how incredible she looked in that slinky, black dress. It set off the ebony color of her hair and complemented the creamy whiteness of her complexion; it brought out her full, rose-petal lips. She looked like a goddess.

"This really is a beautiful home you have, Donovan," she said, looking up at him. "I haven't said it before, but it's very inviting. And this sofa—I could get lost in it."

She stroked the soft upholstery with a graceful hand.

Donovan stood motionless, watching her long slender arm move back and forth across the cushions.

His blood quickened in his veins. What he wouldn't give to be one of those cushions now....

Groping for his equilibrium, he fully entered the room and handed a glass to her, then sat down on the sofa.

"I had a great time tonight," he said. "We should do it again."

She looked at him with those big brown eyes over the rim of her glass as she took the first sip, then set her glass on the coffee table. "I had a nice time, too, but I'm not so sure we should do it again."

"And why is that?" But he knew why.

"Because I wouldn't want us to end up having *too* good a time together."

"I see. Better that we have completely lousy conversations and get on each others nerves every minute of the day?"

She peered down at her glass. "You know what I mean."

He gazed at her feminine profile, feeling the pulse of his heart, the hum of his blood through his body. "No, I don't. Tell me."

He wanted this woman. There was no point denying it. She was the most intriguing creature he'd ever encountered in his life. Brave. Intelligent. Witty. Independent. Unimpressed with the fact that he was a millionaire.

He set down his wine. Reaching one arm across the back of the sofa, he stroked her bare shoulder with a thumb.

She didn't push his hand away; all she did was wet her deliciously full lips, which were already moist from the wine.

"I mean the same thing I've said before," she said. "That you're my client and there's—"

"Something happening between us."

He could see the gentle pulse at her neck begin to beat with fervent intensity. He half expected her to get up off the sofa and walk out on him. But she didn't. For a long, tense few seconds, she just sat there while he stroked her shoulder.

"Yes, there is," she finally said in a breathy voice that sent him hurling over the edge.

He couldn't fight it anymore. Desire was burning through him like an all-encompassing fire. He couldn't remember the last time he'd wanted a woman this badly.

How did she do this to him, and why?

He didn't care why. All he knew was that he had to have her. He had to satisfy this searing need to touch.

Slowly, cautiously, he leaned toward her. Close enough that he could smell the perfumed fragrance of her hair, feel her wine-scented breath against his face.

He hovered there, inches from her lips, waiting to see if she was in agreement, and when she made no move to pull back, he pressed his lips to hers.

Tentatively at first. Exploring. Seeking. Then she let out a soft little erotic whimper that fired his blood to the breaking point.

Her willing response sent a surge of voracious lust whipping through him like a cyclone. He cupped her head in his hands and felt her lips part for him, then he swept his tongue into her hot, wet mouth and deepened the kiss.

She whimpered with pleasure again....

He inched across the sofa, close enough so that he could take all of her into his arms. She melted into him like warm butter, reaching around his shoulders and raking her fingers through his hair. She was bewitching.

He slid his hand down the side of her gown and around her curvaceous bottom, feeling his tuxedo trousers tighten over his growing arousal.

"You taste great," he whispered at her cheek, trailing tiny kisses down to her neck while he shifted her in his arms. She tilted her head back to give him full access, and he devoured as much of her as he could, kissing her bare shoulders and tasting her jawline.

Within seconds, he was easing her onto the soft cushions beneath him, glorying in the potent sensation of her hands tangled in his hair.

She wrapped her legs around his hips, and he settled himself upon her, pressing his erection against her through all their clothing, pulsing his hips and reveling in the unmitigated pleasure of her thrusting her own hips forward in return.

"Mmm," she whispered, kissing him deeply, eating at his mouth as if she'd been starving for him for days, in the same way he'd been starving for her.

A hot, searing flame ignited and flared inside him, followed by something resembling panic. He wasn't sure he'd be able to stop things if they went much further—and he was surprised he'd gotten *this* far. He was dangerously close to the edge of reason. The feel of this woman beneath him was like a tidal wave of undiluted, intoxicating ecstasy storming his senses.

He slid his hand down her thigh and gathered the

fabric of her skirt in his hand, carefully lifting it inch by glorious inch. Her legs were bare beneath the skirt—no stockings—and the warm softness of her smooth leg wrapped around him gave him the most exhilarating palpitations in his chest. Finally, his hand was up under the skirt and at her soft hip, his fingers reaching the narrow band of her bikini panties.

He slid his fingers inside and around to her bottom and she began to kiss him faster, lifting her head off the couch pillows to deepen the kiss.

This was getting out of control. He wanted to make love to her here and now, half-dressed on the sofa, and again afterward in his bed. He brought his hand around to her flat belly, then slid it down to reach inside her panties....

Like a predictable clock chiming midnight, signaling the end of the ball, she squirmed and turned her face away. She pressed a palm to his chest. "Wait. Donovan, we shouldn't be doing this."

He froze, immobilized while his heart continued to pump heated blood through his veins. Closing his eyes for a moment to try to gain control of his breathing, he fought the crippling urge to kiss her again and continue this achingly pleasurable indulgence. He removed his hand from the intimate place it had *almost* been, and sighed.

She shifted slightly beneath him. He recognized her uneasiness—and knowing a woman was uneasy beneath him was about as effective as a bucket of cold water splashing over his head.

He backed off immediately and retreated to his side of the sofa, pushing his hair back off his perspiring forehead. "Sorry." He paused, catching his breath. "I didn't mean to take it that far."

God!

All he'd meant to do was kiss her....

Jocelyn pulled and tugged at the neckline of her gown to try and put herself back together. "It was my fault, too."

An awkward silence ensued.

"Look..."

She didn't let him finish. She stood. "Maybe this was a mistake."

"No, Jocelyn—" She started to leave. "Don't go. Let's talk about this." Damn, he'd really done it now. He followed her down the wide hall.

"There's no point talking," she said. "I knew this was going to happen. I could see it coming, yet I couldn't stop it, and that's dangerous, Donovan. I can't do my job this way. I should resign."

He caught her arm. "Resign! All we did was kiss, really...."

He knew how ridiculous that sounded. It was a hell of a lot more than just a kiss.

"But it might not be just a kiss next time, and where does it go after that? I'll be honest, I'm very attracted to you. So much so, that I'm finding it hard to keep my mind on my work. I'm supposed to be watching you constantly, but I'm not watching you the way I should be. I'm not thinking about potential dangers, I'm thinking about *you*. About how badly I want to..."

Her chest was heaving.

"To what, Jocelyn?"

"To do what we just did."

He released her arm. "I won't lie. I've been thinking about it, too, and it's been getting a little crazy, but please, don't leave. I need you here. At least until the stalker is caught. Then…then maybe we could think about us.''

For a long moment she stood there, staring into his eyes, considering what he'd said.

Please don't leave, he tried to say without words.

But when she spoke, her voice was cool and back under control. His heart sank.

''If it's protection you need, Donovan, I'm no longer the best person for the job. I'm sorry. I'll make the necessary arrangements for another E.P.P., and stay with you until the new operative can take over, but after that, I'm gone. It's for your own safety.''

She went into her room and closed the door behind her.

Donovan backed up against the wall and pinched the bridge of his nose. His chest ached, his safety the last thing on his mind as he thought about what she'd just said, and the fact that she hadn't said a word about the *us* part.

''I'm in trouble, Tess,'' Jocelyn said to her assistant over the phone the next morning, after she escorted Donovan safely to the O.R. She now stood in the waiting room outside. ''I need your help.''

''Why? What's wrong?''

Jocelyn felt some of the tension in her shoulders drain away momentarily. Tess was not only her capable and competent assistant, but her truest confidante and dear friend. She was blond, beautiful, an aerobics fanatic and she'd been with Jocelyn since she'd opened her private agency four years ago. She was a great listener who always told it like it was.

"I gave notice to resign last night," Jocelyn said, "and Dr. Knight needs a new agent immediately."

There was a brief silence on the other end of the line. "What in the world happened? He didn't make a pass at you, did he? Like that slimy old retired senator in New Jersey?"

Jocelyn cupped her forehead with a hand. "No, it wasn't anything like that. Well, it was...I mean, he did make a pass at me, Tess, but the problem was, I was all for it. I think I might have even encouraged him. I'm not sure. I can barely remember what happened. It was all such a blur."

Silence again. "How old is this guy?"

"He's young. Thirty-four, and gorgeous."

"You didn't tell me that!"

"I know. I guess I didn't want to admit that I'd noticed."

She heard Tess take a deep breath and whistle. "As long as I've known you, you've never let this happen. Do you think you're falling for him?"

Jocelyn closed her eyes. "I don't *want* to say yes. I don't want to admit to it or give in to it, but...Lord help me, yes, I think I am. In fact, I think I already have."

"Why don't you want to give in to it? Because he's your client? If that's the problem, we can fix it today. I can find someone else to take over, then you'll be free to go for it."

"No, no, no, I don't *want* to go for it. I want to get as far away from him as possible. I don't want to see him again."

"Why the hell not?"

"Because…" Oh, how could she answer that? It was personal and complicated and would take too long to explain, and it would sound ridiculous. "I just don't want to get involved with anyone right now."

"I'll say it again. *Why the hell not?*"

Why did Tess always insist on acting as her conscience? "Because I'm busy. I don't have time for a relationship."

"That's crap and you know it. You're afraid to get involved with anyone because you're worried he'll be like Tom or your father."

So much for "complicated and too lengthy to explain." Tess hit the mark in one sentence.

That was Tess. Direct and to the point, even when Jocelyn wasn't quite ready to feel the point jabbing her in the behind.

Jocelyn gathered her resolve. "It's not just that. Donovan isn't my type. He's not looking for commitment—he said it himself over dinner last night—and from what I've learned about him, he's never had a serious, long-term relationship with anyone, at least not in his adult life. Why would I want to get involved with someone like that, when the possibility of getting my heart broken is practically a sure thing?"

"Did you ask him why?"

"Why what?"

"Why he's never had a serious relationship with anyone. Maybe he got burned once, too."

"No, I didn't ask."

"Aren't you curious?"

Yes, she was. She was curious about a lot of things.

"I really don't want to ask, because that will only add fuel to the fire. I don't want to get any closer to him. I want to get out of this assignment before I end up in his bed."

"And what would be wrong with that? You're a grown-up, Jocelyn. You deserve a few guilty pleasures every now and then, and you can handle them if you want."

Jocelyn sat down on a chair. "Are you implying what I think you're implying?"

"I'm not implying anything. I'm saying it loud and clear. Do I need a megaphone? If you're attracted to him and he's attracted to you, why not steal a little enjoyment while you can? It wouldn't hurt you to ditch your professional, tough-girl attitude for a night. Especially if we find him another bodyguard. There wouldn't be any ethical problems then."

"You're saying I should have casual sex with him? I'm not good at casual sex. Call me needy, but I have a problem with the 'casual' part."

"Maybe it wouldn't end up casual."

Jocelyn ran a hand through her hair. "I couldn't, Tess. I'm a chicken."

"No, you're not. You're the bravest person I know. Think about what you do for a living. You can tussle with the best of 'em."

"That's different. It's my job."

"So let me get this straight. You're fearless professionally, but scared stiff personally."

Lord, Tess was blunt. It wouldn't be so bad if she wasn't completely bang on.

"Okay, okay, you get the insightful award for today," Jocelyn said, twirling a loose thread from one of her buttonholes around her finger.

"So what do you want me to do?" Tess asked.

Jocelyn considered it a moment, then let out a deep sigh. "Try to find Dr. Knight a new E.P.P., and look into the waiting list to find me a new assignment. Preferably an out-of-town detail."

"So you're not going to take my advice." Tess didn't even try to hide the disappointment in her voice.

Jocelyn stood up to peer through one of the windows on the swinging doors to the O.R. All she saw was her own reflection, which she didn't really want to look at right now.

"Sorry, Tess. I'm not interested in taking risks with my heart. I'll be back in the office as soon as you can get me out of this. The sooner the better."

Jocelyn and Donovan were halfway home when he turned up a side street and pulled over. He turned off the car and draped an arm over the steering wheel, looking at her. "We have to talk."

Heart suddenly racing in her chest, she looked out the windows, checking for cars that might be following them. "There's nothing to talk about, Donovan. My assistant has been working all day to find you another E.P.P."

"No luck?"

"Not yet," she said, still looking out the windows. "So far, the only person available is a guy I don't trust. He's a hothead who would prefer to beat up on an attacker just to prove he's tough, when he should be shielding and evacuating his principal."

"Why won't you look at me?" Donovan asked.

She swallowed nervously. "I'm just trying to do my job."

And I can't bear to look at the tender, pleading expression on your handsome face.

"There's no danger. No one knows we're here," he said.

"Let me be the judge of that."

He sat for a few seconds, waiting for her to assure herself that there were no potential dangers in the neighborhood, then tried again. "You don't have to quit."

"Like I said last night, it's for your own safety."

His gaze was direct and penetrating. "I trust you to take care of that, even after what happened last night."

Jocelyn tried not to notice the way his jeans were pulling tight over his muscular thighs and the way her pulse was thrumming wildly in response. Tried not to think about what Tess had suggested that morning—that Jocelyn go ahead and seek pleasure with her soon-to-be ex-client, for the mere sake of self-indulgence....

"What happened last night *shouldn't* have happened," she said, trying to purge those imprudent, reckless thoughts from her muddled brain. "It's one of the first laws of my profession—*never* get involved with a principal."

He tapped his thumb on the steering wheel and faced forward. "All right, I'll accept that, Jocelyn, because I respect your judgment and your professionalism. If you want to resign and find another E.P.P. for me, that's fine. I'll take another E.P.P. Maybe it *would* be best."

That seemed a little too easy, but she suspected it was merely the calm before the storm....

Donovan shifted on the leather seat to face her. "Last night was incredible, Jocelyn."

Oh, God.

"It took every ounce of self-control I possessed," he continued, "not to follow you into your room after what happened, and pick up where we left off, when I knew I should be promising never to do it again. If I thought I could make that promise, I would try harder to convince you to stay, because I am completely willing to place my life in your hands. But I'm not that strong, Jocelyn. I can't make that promise. I wanted you last night like I've never wanted any woman in my life, and that feeling's not going away. I was in agony today. Agony. I can't fight it, nor can I resist touching you if you're anywhere within reach."

I'm within reach now, she thought, struggling with feelings of desire and longing that were bombarding her senses and becoming impossible to ignore.

Why did he have to smell so good? Look so good? Sound so good? The moist texture of his mouth, his lips parting seductively, and the heated glimmer in his eye—it was all so erotically, achingly sweet. Here in the car, she didn't feel like a bodyguard...she felt like a woman. A woman tingling all over. A woman struggling to resist the power of this man's appeal.

Her breaths came in short little gasps. They stared at each other for a long, pulse-pounding moment.

This was insane.

"If I could resist you," he said, "I would. The unfortunate thing is, I can't."

He swayed toward her, just a little, and it was enough to break down every wall of defense she had tried to build around herself today while he was operating on people. Her cover came crumbling down in a great, chaotic descent.

Donovan cupped her cheek in his hand and gazed at her for a shuddering instant before he pressed his mouth to hers.

The world spun stormily around Jocelyn as she reached her arms around this man who drove her wild in the most ground-shifting way. He somehow managed to make her forget who she was and what she was doing here. All that mattered was the erotic delight of his hands touching her.

The drenching heat of arousal between her thighs hit like a tidal surge.

He whispered in her ear. "Come home with me, Jocelyn." Gooseflesh tickled down her body and caused another wave of creamy heat between her legs. "I want you in my bed...."

Tess's words resounded in her mind again: *Why not steal a little enjoyment while you can?*

Lord, how she wanted to...

He kissed her neck and stroked her shoulders and back, then devoured her mouth again with another skillfully wet kiss that dissolved most of what was left of her resistance. She wanted this man inside her, and she didn't care what the consequences were. Surely she could deal with her fears another day.

Then she heard laughter from somewhere outside her hazy consciousness, somewhere outside the car. She pulled back and turned. Two teenagers were standing outside her window, watching them! How long had they been there?

Realizing they'd been discovered, the youths immediately turned and took off down the street, but the damage was already done. Jocelyn had fallen down in her duties, to an unimaginable degree.

"They're gone," Donovan whispered, leaning forward to continue kissing her, but she held him back with a hand.

"No, that was a sign."

"Don't tell me you're superstitious now."

"No, I'm *awake* now, thank God. What if that had been your stalker? This is crazy, Donovan, and you know it."

He grabbed hold of the steering wheel with both hands and tapped his forehead against it. "This *is* crazy. It's a good thing you resigned, because if you didn't I'd have to fire you. Because I don't want you as my bodyguard anymore. I want you as a woman. In my bed."

"That can't happen." She tried to fight her impossible desires. "Not yet. Not now."

"But someday? Can I at least entertain some hopes?"

She couldn't seem to answer right away. What just happened had spooked her, doused her with a healthy splash of reality. Her heart was racing inside her chest. Besides that, she wasn't sure she could handle this with Donovan, not if it was going to blow up in her face in a month's time.

At her hesitation, his eyes narrowed, then he blew out a breath of air. "I need a second or two to get a hold of myself." He flicked the latch on the door and got out.

"No, wait! Donovan!" She got out, too, meeting him around the front of the vehicle and taking him by the arm. "Get back in the car. I can't be sure we're safe here."

Just then, a navy blue sedan came speeding out from behind the car that was parked to the rear of them. Jocelyn's senses thrummed to life, and she pulled Donovan across the sidewalk to the shelter of a huge oak tree. She shielded his body with hers, just as the driver opened fire out of the passenger side window.

Seven

Tree bark exploded beside Jocelyn's head, then tires squealed and the car sped off. She tried to see the license plate, but it was too late.

Donovan stepped back onto the sidewalk, staring after the attacker.

"Get in the car," Jocelyn ordered. "I'll drive."

She flipped open her cell phone to call the police as she ran around the front of the vehicle. She had the emergency number on speed dial. She gave the particulars about the assailant while she got in and started the engine. "You better buckle up," she said.

Donovan watched her squeal out onto the road. "What the hell just happened?"

"We were being watched, and not just by those teenagers. Look out the rear window. Did he come back around? Are we being followed?"

"No, there's no one behind us."

She pulled a U-turn and started back in the other direction, got onto the main road and shifted quickly in and out of lanes.

Donovan kept one hand on the dash to brace himself. "You're quite a driver."

"Comes with the territory. Anybody else shifting around behind us?"

He turned to look. "No. It's clear."

She turned left at a busy intersection and went up and down some side streets to avoid the direct route home. They finally reached his building, and Jocelyn parked out back instead of in his usual spot inside the garage. She escorted him out of the car quickly and skirted through a back entrance for which she had a key.

"I didn't even know this door was here," Donovan said. "You did your homework, didn't you?"

"Preparation is everything." She checked around corners in basement halls, moving quickly to the elevator and keeping an eye out until he was safely inside. They rode up the twenty-two floors in complete silence.

Jocelyn took all possible precautions entering Donovan's penthouse and locking the door behind them. She searched the place, then closed all the blinds and curtains and told Donovan to stay away from the windows.

Once they were sure they were out of immediate danger, Jocelyn led the way into the kitchen where Donovan sat on one of the stools at the center island.

"Are you all right?" she asked. "Can I get you anything? A glass of water?"

"That would be great, thanks. Things were pretty nutty back there."

She went to fill a glass from the water cooler in the corner. "This is obviously a very determined stalker, and what happened today will happen again and again until he's caught, so I want to do everything I can to assist the police in their investigation." She set the glass of water down in front of him. "They're going to be here soon, so let's try again to figure out who would want to hurt you. We need to give the police something more to work with. You mentioned the grief counseling center you're working on. You don't have any plans to pave over a park or anything like that, do you?"

"No, the location hasn't even been decided yet. We're still in the fund-raising stage."

"What else can you think of? Have you lost any patients lately? Could there be a grieving loved one who blames you?"

"I guess it's possible. I'm a good surgeon, but I'm not God. I've lost my share."

"Can you get me their names? Maybe the police could look into it."

He nodded.

Jocelyn flipped open her phone to call the police and see if they'd apprehended anyone. Unfortunately they hadn't, which was not surprising, since the assailant had sped off too quickly and she hadn't identified the plate number.

She was told an officer would be there soon to ask questions, and that they would be heightening the investigation.

Two hours later, after Jocelyn had dealt with the police and called Tess to report what had happened, she found Donovan in the kitchen, cooking.

She took a seat on one of the stools. "How are you doing?"

He stood over the stovetop on the island, whisking something in a saucepan. He wore his faded jeans and a white T-shirt, tucked in.

"Better," he replied. "Cooking relaxes me. Want some bacon-wrapped scallops?" He set down the whisk, opened one of the stainless steel ovens behind him, and pulled out a pan of sizzling hors d'oeuvres. He set them on a china platter, and after sticking toothpicks in them, set the platter in front of Jocelyn.

"Don't mind if I do. Oh, sweet heaven, these are delicious." Then she realized how hot they were and opened her mouth to wave a hand in front of her face. "Ow."

Donovan smiled as he returned to his whisking. "Burn yourself? If only you would exercise such a lack of caution and restraint with me."

She couldn't help smiling. "I'm sorry, Donovan, but you have to admit I'm right. Especially after today."

He whisked faster. "Yes, and I must say, you were pretty impressive driving my car." He lifted his sexy gaze. "You, my dear, are no debutante."

She laughed. "And you, kind sir, are an excellent cook." She popped another tender, juicy scallop into her mouth. "What are you making?"

"Grilled chicken with lemon cream sauce over angel hair pasta, and sautéed snow peas. Are you hungry?"

"I'm starved and that sounds amazing. We forgot to eat dinner, didn't we? For obvious reasons, I guess."

He tilted his head, not bothering to speak about why.

"Listen…Donovan," she said cautiously, "before we sit down to eat, I'd like to clear the air about what happened today."

His gaze lifted again. "I got shot at by a stalker."

"Before that."

"You mean what attracted the voyeuristic teenagers? Yeah, that was interesting, too, wasn't it?"

"It was more than interesting," she replied, feeling like she was treading into dangerous territory, but needing to get this out in the open so it wouldn't happen again. "It was excruciating."

He set the saucepan aside and flicked off the burner. Slowly, sensuously, he moved toward her like a confident panther on the prowl. Her blood began to race faster through her veins.

"In what way was it excruciating?" He took her hand and pulled her gently to her feet. She stared at him for a shaky moment while he raised her hand to his lips and kissed her knuckles. Tremors of delight danced across her skin.

"In *that* way."

His wicked gaze met hers.

"You're cruel, Donovan," she said in a low, breathy voice while she tried to fight the powerful emotions that were tugging at her from all directions.

"No more cruel than you are, not allowing me to have hope."

She swallowed over the huge lump of anxiety in her throat. "We shouldn't be thinking about this kind of thing right now."

"You're the one who brought it up."

This was agonizing. "Yes, I did, because I thought

we should—'' He laid a few more soft kisses upon her knuckles, and the cool, lingering moisture from his lips seemed to tingle all the way up her arm. She forgot what she was going to say. Damn him....

''You thought we should clear the air,'' he said for her.

''Yes.'' *Thank you.*

''Let's clear it, then. I promise I'll be good.'' He gave her hand back to her and let his own hands fall to his sides. ''I'm listening.''

Her heart did a few wild little somersaults in her chest. How was it possible that he could reduce her to a stammering idiot, when she'd promised herself she would be a brick wall?

''I know I said I was going to resign,'' she told him, ''but in light of what happened today, and the fact that Tess can't seem to find anyone to replace me on such short notice, I think it's important for me to stay on for a little while.''

He wet his too-inviting lips. ''Ah. I suppose the next thing you're going to tell me is that the kissing has to stop.''

''Precisely.'' She waited with apprehension for his argument, prepared her rebuttals in her mind....

''Done,'' he said flatly.

She shook her head in disbelief; her voice revealed her utter amusement. ''Done? I don't believe you.''

He laid his hand on his chest, looking dismayed by her lack of confidence in his ability to keep his hands to himself. ''You don't trust me.''

''I do trust you, it's just that...well, you haven't exactly been agreeable to my requests before now.''

He considered her point. ''Maybe not, but I've had

some time to think about things, and I feel differently about everything tonight.''

''Differently? How so?''

''I realize that in addition to the fact that I'm your client, and the fact that I was shot at today and you feel responsible, you're nervous about getting involved with me because you don't know me very well and you're afraid I might turn out to be the playboy you thought I was when you first met me. A little more time together will give me the chance to prove to you that you're wrong. And maybe prove it to myself, too.''

The last thing he said went straight through her. He was revealing something of himself. A deeper vulnerability. A desire to improve some of his shortcomings.

She hadn't imagined he was aware that he even had any.

''So you're going to be good?'' she replied, trying to recapture the mood from a few minutes ago—when it was a little more simple. A little more casual. ''You're not going to try to tempt me?''

He touched her chin briefly. ''I'm going to do my very best, hoping of course, that there will be a reward at the end.''

''Like a dog treat?'' she replied, finding this all very hard to believe.

''No.'' He backed away and opened the oven to serve up dinner. ''Like your heart.''

A ripple of unwelcome anticipation coursed through Jocelyn. *My heart?*

Damn him for being so impossibly, wonderfully charming.

* * *

They ate dinner by candlelight in the formal dining room, on the shiny, polished mahogany table, and sipped sparkling, alcohol-free cranberry cocktail from crystal goblets. After the dishes were cleared, it was past ten o'clock.

"One last chance," Jocelyn said, "to cancel your surgery tomorrow morning. We could stay here and watch TV and avoid risks."

"I would if I could, but it's an important procedure. It's not something that should be postponed."

She nodded, helping him load the dishwasher. A few minutes later, they were yawning.

"Will you be able to sleep?" she asked.

He walked her to her bedroom door. "I doubt it."

"Would you like to stay up a little longer? We could watch a movie if it would help."

"No, I have to be in the O.R. at 6:00 a.m. I should at least try to get some shut-eye."

"All right. Well, don't worry. I'm here, and remember I sleep with one eye open, the monitor's on and your new alarm system is second to none. You'll be fine tonight."

He settled one broad shoulder against her door-jamb, and relaxed there, just looking at her. "Will I?"

Jocelyn's insides began to quiver at the awesome effect of his words in the wake of his sexy green eyes, half-shuttered in the dim light.

"Of course," she replied, even though she knew he was referring to another kind of danger. The kind that went hand in hand with temptations and consequences.

His voice was calm and soothing after the madness of the day. "I'm sure you're right."

Still, he remained at her door, gazing into her eyes, then down at her lips, back up to her eyes again.

"You're hovering," she said in a playful tone. "Remember what you promised."

"I promised I wouldn't kiss you. I didn't promise I wouldn't look at you. It's not easy to pry my eyes away, you know."

"Well, you'd better if you're going to be able to keep them open during surgery in the morning."

He visibly snapped himself out of it, and stepped away from the doorjamb. "You're right, you're right. I should go." He started to back away. "Thanks, Jocelyn."

"For what?"

He paused in the hall. "For being here."

"It's my job."

"No, it's more than that. You make me feel…" He shrugged, starting to back away again. "Happy. I've never been so happy to have a woman stay over-night, when there wasn't any chance of you know what."

"Parcheesi?"

He laughed. "Is that what they call it these days?"

"God only knows."

He laughed again, still backing away. "You're adorable, you know."

Jocelyn began to close her door. "Good night, Doctor."

"And you're breaking my heart."

"While you're breaking a promise. Good night," she repeated, closing her door until it clicked, but remaining there with her ear against it, just to hear the sound of his footfalls until they disappeared into his room.

* * *

At 3:00 a.m., Jocelyn awoke to a knock at her door. "Yes?"

Donovan answered from the hall. "You awake?"

Her shoulders heaved with a sigh, and she climbed out of bed and opened the door to find him standing there looking sleepy, disheveled and delicious, shirtless with nothing on but a pair of black pajama bottoms.

"I woke you, didn't I?"

"It's okay. I had to get up to answer your knock on my door anyway."

He smiled, and she wasn't quite sure how she'd managed to speak, with that smooth, golden chest at eye level, scrambling her senses into a jumbled mess.

She noticed his eyes were bloodshot. "Can't sleep?"

"I haven't gotten a wink so far. I think it was everything that happened today. I'm still wired."

"I know the feeling. What can I do? Want some hot milk or something?"

"Hot milk? What, am I twelve?"

"You don't drink hot milk?"

He raised his eyebrows and shook his head. "I didn't think *anybody* drank hot milk. At least not since the fifties."

"I do, and it works. Truly." She started toward the kitchen. "Come on, I'll prove it to you."

They both walked barefoot to the kitchen and turned on the lights. Jocelyn poured some milk into a mug and stuck it in the microwave. While the appliance hummed, she explained the hot milk technique.

"If you want it to work, you have to make sure you close your eyes as soon as the sleepy feeling hits, because if you don't, you'll miss it. It's like a wave you have to catch. So you shouldn't drink it in the living room, because then you'll have to get up and go to bed, and that alone might make you miss the wave. Drink it in bed.''

"I see. Sounds like you've got it down to a science.''

"I do.'' The microwave beeped, and she removed the steaming cup and stirred it with a spoon. ''There you go.''

He took the cup and smelled it. ''Hot milk. Hmm.''

She put her hand on his back to usher him to bed, and the warm feel of his well-toned muscles beneath her fingertips sent shivers up and down her spine. She tried to ignore them, but it was no use. She gave up trying, and resolved to go back to her own bed ASAP.

They reached his bedroom, and she hesitated for a fraction of a second before going with him inside. She'd never escorted a principal to bed before—and certainly not a principal who looked like Donovan, bare-chested and devastatingly masculine in nothing but his drawstring pajama bottoms. It would never have seemed appropriate with any of her previous clients, nor had any of them ever attempted to push the boundaries like Donovan did.

Still, his comfort and safety were her concern, so she entered the room. ''You'll be all right now?'' she asked, pausing at the bottom of the king-size bed while he set the mug on his side table and climbed in.

"I don't know. It depends on the hot milk.''

She was about to say good-night when he gestured

toward the chair in the corner. "Have a seat. Stay and talk to me for a few minutes. Tell me something personal."

She swallowed nervously. "Like what?"

"I don't know. Like what kind of person you were in high school. Were you popular—you know, the student council type, the prom queen—or did you hang out with the druggies?"

Jocelyn moved to the chair and sat down. "I wasn't anything. I just went to class, got average grades, had a few friends I hung out with most of the time."

"Your basic invisible kid, ignored for being normal," he said, a little too perceptively. "Did you have any boyfriends? Or was the social climbing med student your one and only love?"

"No, I didn't have any boyfriends in high school. I had a couple of guys who were friends, and we hung out some times, but I didn't even go to the prom. None of us did. Looking back on it, maybe we were geeks. I was a bit of a loner. Still am."

"But why? You're gorgeous and funny. You should have been snapped up by now."

She sat forward. "It's simpler this way. I've gotten used to living alone and I like to focus all my energy on my work. I don't have to worry about disappointing anyone when I don't come home for weeks on end. But hey, who are you to point the finger, Mr. Single-Man."

He took the first sip of his milk. "Point taken, but I've had some really good excuses. First it was medical school, which kept me busy constantly, then there were years of residencies, where I was sleep-deprived and stressed out most of the time. I haven't had time for a relationship.''

''What about now? You've been here in Chicago for a couple of years, and you appear to have a social life. You go to the theater and you have women calling you.''

He took another sip. ''Yeah, but I never really got to know any of them.''

''Who's fault is that?''

He gave her a playful look. ''It couldn't be mine. I'm perfect, don't ya know.''

Jocelyn smiled.

''Seriously though,'' he continued, taking another sip from his mug, ''I know I haven't seemed like much of a family guy, and maybe I'm not. I've been on my own for a long time.''

''You must have some family. Brothers? Sisters?''

He shook his head. ''I'm an only child. Not that my parents ever intended it to be that way. They died when I was two.''

A flash of grief flared through her. ''I'm so sorry, Donovan. I didn't know. I mean, I knew they weren't alive, but I didn't know when you lost them. What happened?''

He gazed at his mug as he spoke. ''Car accident. I was in the back seat, and we hit a patch of ice and went over a low cliff. Somehow I survived, and someone heard me crying the next morning. A woman found me outside the car, sitting in the dirt, suffering symptoms of exposure. My parents had been dead all night. It's a miracle I survived.''

''My God, do you remember any of it?''

''No. I barely remember my parents, though my grandmother raised me and always talked about them. She was good to me. She died when I was seventeen and I received my inheritance then, which—aside from a small monthly allowance for my upbringing—had been held in trust. This penthouse was part of it. My parents had bought it together when they married, and wanted to spend their lives here. I lived in it with them when I was very small, before they died. Then, like the rest of the estate, it was held in trust. So you see, I didn't always have money, and I didn't ask for it, nor do I consider it a part of who I am. I'd give it all away this minute to have my parents back.''

Jocelyn's whole body ached with empathy for Donovan's loss and his lifelong yearning. She had already realized that he wasn't shallow. This only reconfirmed it. ''I had no idea. What about becoming a doctor? When did you decide to do that?''

''I always knew that's what I wanted to do. Unlike your ex, it wasn't because I wanted a fancy penthouse or expensive car. I think it was because I wanted to feel like I had some control over saving people's lives, because I sure as hell felt powerless after I lost my parents. I didn't know why I had been so lucky to be spared, and wanted to give something back and make my survival worthwhile. So I used part of the inheritance to put myself through medical school. When I was finished my residencies, that's when I came back here to live. It was kind of strange—like coming home, even though I barely remember living here when I was little.'' He was quiet for a moment. ''Too bad air bags weren't standard back then. They might have lived.''

Jocelyn got up and went to sit beside him on the bed. She reached forward and stroked the hair off his forehead, then cupped his cheek with her hand. "I'm so sorry that happened to you."

"Me, too. From what I heard, my parents were great people."

She rubbed his forehead again. "Is that why you're trying to raise money for the grief counseling center for children?"

"Yeah. I know what it can do to a child. The fears and the grief, the abandonment issues and survivor guilt." He finished the last of his hot milk and sat forward to set the mug on his side table. When he reached across, she saw there was not only a scar on his shoulder—which she had noticed when they'd gone running that first day—but more scars under his arm, along his ribs.

She reached to touch them while he was still leaning. "That's two car accidents you've been in. These look like they were serious."

He raised his arm to inspect them himself. "They've healed nicely though, don't you think?"

"I guess so." She continued to touch them, feeling the warmth of his skin, wanting very badly to rub away the pain he must have suffered, both as a child and a year ago when he'd been hit by that other car. "You said a woman went through a red light and rammed you?"

"Yeah."

"Did she live?"

"No. She wasn't wearing a seat belt."

Jocelyn considered that. "Was she drunk?"

"No. Apparently she and her husband had just had a fight, and she was pretty messed up."

Jocelyn continued to touch the scars, tilting her

head to the side as she stared down at them. "What was the date of the accident?"

He told her.

"That's exactly a year to the day before the intruder broke into your house and left you the letter. You don't suppose…"

Donovan sat forward. "That the husband has it out for me?"

"It's a possibility." Jocelyn went to get her phone. "I'll leave a voice mail message with the cop who was here today and have him check it out."

She made the phone call from the kitchen, then returned to Donovan's bedroom. She was about to tell him not to think about it anymore, to try to get some sleep, but she didn't have to.

She approached the bed. His eyes were closed, his breathing deep and heavy.

"See? Hot milk works." She bent forward and placed a gentle kiss on his forehead.

She pulled the covers up over his legs and watched him for a moment, gazing at the perfection of his face—the strong line of his jaw, the straightness of his nose, the beauty of his eyes, even when they were closed.

He was handsome, yes, but there was so much more to him than that, she thought, her heart still aching from what he'd told her about his parents.

She imagined him making the decision to start a grief counseling clinic for children. He must have spent his whole life pondering and mulling over his childhood and upbringing, longing for what had been taken from him, and wishing someone had been able to ease the pain. Now, he wanted to help other children, to help ease *their* pain.

Jocelyn swallowed over the huge lump in her throat. There was a very big heart in there, she realized, gazing down at Donovan's chest, fighting the urge to lay her hand upon his skin and feel his heart beating. It was a fragile, wounded heart that had never found the courage to love anyone. It was no wonder. *I know what it can do to a child. The fears and the grief, the abandonment issues.*

She suddenly understood what he'd meant earlier that night, when he'd said he wanted to prove to himself that he wasn't a playboy. He obviously had some understanding of the damage done to his heart, and blamed that for his single lifestyle.

Feeling suddenly sleepy, Jocelyn pulled the covers up to Donovan's shoulders and turned from the room. Something tugged inside her—an intense, aching desire that shot through her soul like a rocket. A desire to protect this man, no matter what it took, no matter how long.

Never in her career had she experienced anything like it.

Eight

The next night, they returned home to Donovan's penthouse after a long, stressful day at the hospital. Stressful for Donovan, because of the two back-to-back surgeries, and stressful for Jocelyn, who didn't relax or let down her guard, even for a minute, grilling everyone and anyone who wanted to get within ten paces of Donovan, and constantly watching over her shoulder. Realizing her limitations, she had called Tess to look into retaining a few more operatives to make this a team detail and increase security temporarily, at least until they gained some leads on the stalker.

Shortly after they entered the penthouse, the phone rang. "I'll get it." Jocelyn answered the telephone in the front hall. "Hello? Sergeant O'Reilly, have you learned anything?"

Donovan approached, watching her and waiting,

curious about what the police had managed to discover during the day.

"I see." She looked at Donovan. "Yes. We were lucky. I'm not sure yet. Yes, I'll do that. Thank you for letting me know." She hung up the phone.

"What happened?"

Jocelyn moved toward him and placed her hand on his arm. "You won't believe what I'm going to tell you. Maybe we should go and sit down."

She led the way into the living room, where they both sat on the sofa. Jocelyn took Donovan's hand in hers, and held it. "The man whose wife died in that car accident is the man who's stalking you. His name is Ben Cohen."

For a long time, Donovan gazed at her. "How do the police know?"

"Because after I gave them the information, they went to his apartment to question him. He wasn't there, but the landlady told them some things that gave them enough reason to get a search warrant, and when they got inside, they found pictures of you on his wall, newspaper articles about the accident, pictures of your smashed SUV, among other things."

"Did they arrest him?

"That's the problem. He wasn't there, and he hadn't been there for a while. The landlady said a week or two. The police don't know where he is. He hasn't been to work in a week, either. Hasn't even called in sick."

"It sounds like he *wants* people to know he's the one."

"Yes, which makes him all the more dangerous, because he has no fear. This is a personal vendetta for him, and he doesn't care about the consequences.

He doesn't seem to care that he's going to lose his job or his apartment, and most likely go to prison.''

Donovan cupped his forehead in his hand and squeezed his pounding temples. ''The accident wasn't even my fault. *She* was the one who ran the red light.''

''I know, but he's obviously not rational. He wants someone to blame, and from what the police found in his apartment, he's angry about the issue of SUVs being like tanks on the roads. He thinks it's a conspiracy to wipe out the lower classes, and the fact that you're a rich doctor only added fuel to that fire.''

''This is crazy!'' He stood up and paced around the living room. ''I didn't get an SUV to kill people! I got it because it was good in the snow and in my line of work—trying to *save* people—I can't afford to get stuck on the way to the hospital.''

''I know, I know,'' Jocelyn said, rising to her feet and going to his side. ''None of this is your fault. He's a nut, but at least we know who he is and the police are keeping an eye out for him. They'll catch him. It won't take long.''

''But in the meantime? Am I supposed to go about my life, waiting to get shot at again?''

She took his hand in hers. ''No. You're not supposed to go about your life, not if I have any say in the matter.''

He met her gaze directly. ''What are you suggesting?''

''It's my job to protect you, Donovan, and the risk-level—now that we know what's going on—has skyrocketed in the past twenty-four hours. You can't continue to do the things you normally do, because he's been watching, waiting for the chance to strike—like yesterday on the sidewalk. I don't want you to be a sitting duck. I want you to come away with me.''

"I can't tell you where I'm going,'' Donovan said to his friend, Dr. Mark Reeves, over the phone, "because I don't know. She won't tell me.''

"I had no idea it would get this serious,'' Mark said. "I half thought the intruder was a burglar, like the police wanted to believe, and thought maybe the letter was unconnected. Or maybe I was just hoping.''

"Look, don't worry. Jocelyn is a professional. She knows what she's doing and I have complete faith in her.''

"So you're on a first-name basis,'' his friend said with a curious tone.

Mark was single, but didn't have many women in his life. Not that he didn't have his share of females trying to bang down his door. He was just too busy with his work to stop and smell the roses. Which was why he enjoyed hearing about all of Donovan's dates. Donovan supposed it was Mark's way of having a vicarious love life.

"You're not just making this up, are you?'' Mark said. "So you can take off with her on a wild Jamaican weekend while I cover your patients?''

Donovan rolled his eyes toward the ceiling. "No, Mark.''

"Don't fault me. A guy can't help wondering. She's a looker, and I've seen the way you looked at each other at the hospital. There's heat between you—the sizzling kind. Is she still sleeping in the guest bedroom?''

The direction of the conversation unnerved Donovan suddenly. He tried to laugh it off. "Mark, you need to get a life. I've got to go."

"But wait, why won't you tell me anything?"

Donovan considered that with more than a little profundity. Why wouldn't he say anything? Because this was deeper and more personal than any affair he'd had in his past? Because he didn't want to jinx it? Or because he himself was still completely in the dark about what was going on?

"This is different, that's all," he replied with the intention of being vague. "She's my bodyguard, and just for the record, she *is* still in the guest room."

Mark whistled. "No kidding. She must be pretty tough. I haven't known a woman yet who's been able to resist you."

"Well, she is an original, that's for sure. I've never met a woman like her."

Mark's voice lowered. "I was right. There *is* something going on between you. Just tell me this, are you going to lure her out of the guest room any time soon?"

Donovan stared down at the dial pad on the phone, shaking his head at his friend's typical tenacity. *I'm doing my best,* he thought.

"Enough nosy questions, Mark. My kiss-and-tell days are over. Thanks for covering my patients, and I'll see you when I get back."

Donovan hung up the phone, anxious to get on the road with Jocelyn, to wherever they were going. He was looking forward to being alone with her. Somewhere safe, where she would be able to relax a little and, for once, let down her guard.

He didn't mean professionally.

* * *

After a long, careful trip out of Chicago in a rented car under Tess's name, Jocelyn turned up the winding, woodsy road that led to the cabin. No one would ever be able to trace them here, and it had the added benefit of being familiar to Jocelyn, who had come here twice before. It was the perfect hideout.

They drove through the shady woods for a few miles, churning up dust on the dry road while rays of sunshine gleamed like dappled light through the trees.

Donovan looked out the window. "This is really isolated. "You're sure we'll be safe here?"

Safe from the stalker, yes. Safe from her growing attraction to Donovan? Not likely, considering this was probably the most romantic place on earth.

"Positive." She tried to sound confident and ignore her personal feelings. "No one knows where we are, and I took the necessary precautions when we left the city."

They finally pulled up in front of a cedar, prow-fronted cabin overlooking a lake, with huge floor-to-ceiling windows and a multilevel deck with patio furniture, a round table with a sun umbrella and a barbecue. Rich green grass went all the way down to the water, where a small cruiser was tied up at a private wharf.

"This is beautiful," Donovan said. "You sure know how to pick a spot."

"Well, I figured if we're going to be forced to leave town and be inconvenienced by Cohen, we might as well at least be comfortable, and maybe even enjoy ourselves."

Enjoy ourselves. She shouldn't have said that. It

inspired all kinds of inappropriate images in her mind.

Jocelyn turned off the car. The silence was astonishing. All they could hear was a single bird chirping, and the sound of a light breeze whispering through the pines and leafy elms.

Donovan stared up at the cabin. ''You've been here before?''

''Twice, yes. Wait till you see the inside.''

They opened their doors and breathed in the clean scent of the woods, then stepped onto a carpet of soft, brown pine needles in the driveway. Fetching their bags out of the trunk, they made their way up to the door, where the key and a welcome note from the owners were waiting for them in the wooden mailbox. Jocelyn opened the door and let Donovan enter first before following him inside.

Nothing had changed since the last time she'd been here. Everything was rustic pine—the kitchen table and chairs, the hutch full of china, the plank floor and the pine walls, as well as the honey-pine ceiling, supported by solid cedar timbers.

''Wow,'' Donovan said, looking up at the cathedral ceiling in the great room and the huge, gray stone fireplace. ''Looks like we're going to get that vacation we've both been needing. How long do we get to stay?''

She set down her bag. ''That depends on how long it takes the police to find Cohen. Could be twenty-four hours, could be a month.''

''Let's hope it's a month. Though I doubt the hospital would be happy about that.''

Jocelyn locked the door behind them. ''Come on, I'll show you the bedrooms.''

"A woman after my own heart," he said.

Fighting the thrill that charged through her like an electric current, Jocelyn poked him in the chest. She couldn't afford to be knocked off-kilter by something as minor as a suggestive joke. "Behave yourself, Doctor. Our rooms are on opposite sides of the cabin."

Gathering her composure, she picked up her bag and led the way across the open concept kitchen and living area, to the bedroom on the ground floor. A four-poster pine bed stood against the wall; white wicker furniture was arranged in a corner beside the glass sliding doors that led out onto a deck.

"I'll take this room," she said, then led him across to the other side of the cabin, where they climbed stairs to a loft.

The master suite had its own balcony and private bath, as well as a skylight over the bed.

Donovan set down his bag. "That'll be great for stargazing."

"For sure. You'll be comfortable enough here?"

He walked to the bed and pressed his hands onto the mattress. "Well, let me see…nice and firm. It's perfect. Want to come try it out?"

She laughed. "I'll trust your diagnosis, Doctor, and stay on this side of the room, thank you very much. Besides, I've already tried it out, the last time I was here."

His eyes narrowed playfully. "Alone, I hope."

Jocelyn folded her arms over her chest. "That is none of your business."

He raised his hands in mock surrender. "You're right, I'm sorry. I'd just like to know you better, that's all, and I'm curious about certain things."

She gazed at him intently. "About what, exactly?"

"About your life before I met you. Did you bring other clients here? Or were you here just for pleasure?"

Jocelyn sighed, wishing she didn't feel so inclined to answer his questions, wishing that this desire to be closer to him on an emotional level would go away. But ever since the night in his bedroom, when he'd told her about his past and she'd told him things about her personal life, she'd felt more connected to him. She had felt like she was talking to a friend she'd known for years.

"I wouldn't exactly call it pleasure," she replied, "but it wasn't for work reasons, either."

He sauntered toward her. "Now you've got me *really* curious. You can't leave me hanging."

Her pulse began to race as he approached, stopping in front of her, close enough that she could smell his musky male scent. Oh, this was going to be a very difficult assignment over the next few days....

"All right, I'll tell you. I came here the first time with my mother when I was fourteen, just after my father left us. She wanted to get away, so she wouldn't have to answer the phone and explain to everyone what had happened. We stayed for two weeks. Then I came back alone, years later, after Tom and I broke up."

Donovan stared at her for a long moment. "So this place doesn't exactly have pleasant memories for you."

She shook her head.

"Why did you choose it?"

"Because it was the safest place I knew, and I'd basically already done the advance. I know the layout of the property and the inside of the cabin like the back of my hand."

"Always a professional," he said.

"I try."

He gazed at her pensively for a few more seconds, then thankfully dropped the subject. She had the feeling, however, that it would come up again at some point....

"Want to get the groceries out of the car?" he asked.

"Sure." Jocelyn led the way down the stairs.

They brought in the food—a week's supply that Tess had picked up for them and delivered just before they left Chicago in the middle of the night. They stowed it away in the fridge and cupboards.

"What would you like for dinner tonight?" Donovan asked, checking out the cooking utensils in the drawers. "I don't want to influence you, but I make a perfect barbecued steak."

"Sounds great."

If his steak was half as good as his chicken and lemon sauce, and he continued to be such an enjoyable dinner companion, Jocelyn was going to find it very difficult to remember that she was not here on a quest for pleasure. Epicurean or otherwise. She was here to do a job.

That evening after dinner, they walked down to the beach. The water was calm, except for tiny, circular ripples from fish bobbing to the surface. The sun was setting just beyond the treeline on the other side of the lake.

It was a hot night, so Jocelyn had changed into a black T-shirt and khaki walking shorts with Nike sandals, but Donovan still wore his jeans. Jocelyn spread a blanket on the sand.

"Listen to the crickets," he said. "What a gorgeous night."

He began to unbutton his shirt.

"What do you think you're doing?"

He unbuttoned it all the way down and shrugged out of it, then hopped on one foot while he pulled off a shoe. "I'm checking out the lake."

"Are you wearing a swimsuit under those?" she asked, pointing to his jeans, trying not to stare at the sheer magnificence of his bare chest in the glimmering, red twilight.

"Nope." He pulled off the other shoe.

"Hold on a second!" Jocelyn blurted out, realizing what he was doing. "You can't do that here!"

"Why not? It's a scorcher tonight, and there's no one here but us."

"*Us* being the operative word! I'm here, and I don't particularly want to see your—"

Good God.

He pulled down his jeans, and she caught a flash of his bare hip just before she shut her eyes and whirled around to face the other direction. The next thing she heard was the sound of bare feet running onto the wharf and a huge, resounding splash.

Jocelyn opened her eyes, turned and looked down at Donovan's clothes on the blanket at her feet.

All of them.

Right down to the baby blue boxers.

She walked to the edge of the wharf just as Donovan resurfaced. "The water's great!" He flipped his wet hair back off his face. He was one beautiful man. "You gotta come in!"

"I will most certainly *not* come in!"

He laughed. "Why not? It's a gorgeous night, Miss Executive Protection Professional. There's no one here. Relax for once, just for a little while."

"I've said it before and I'll say it again, Donovan—that's precisely when something would happen—as soon as I relaxed in my duties. You've hired me to do a job, and I intend to do it. I'll watch."

She chose not to tell him that watching felt equally as dangerous. For her, anyway.

"Have it your way."

He dove under the water, and she saw more than she wanted to see—a tight, muscular bare butt to die for. Her insides quivered with excitement. Was he trying to drive her mad on purpose? She cupped her forehead in her hand and shut her eyes again.

Feeling slightly desperate, she glanced all around, looking for anybody who might suddenly appear for some unknown reason. The owners, perhaps? A lost hiker? Of course there was no one—it was only wishful thinking on her part—so she looked back down at Donovan, frolicking in the water and damn well driving her insane with both exasperation and yearning.

He treaded water and looked up at her with a tempting smile. "Sure you won't change your mind?"

"I'm sure." But she wasn't sure. What she really wanted to do was dive into that lake and cool off. Because she sure as hell needed to.

"I can see you're changing your mind," he said teasingly, still treading water.

How in God's name did he know that? she wondered miserably. Was it written on her forehead in great big letters—I'm Hot For You, Doctor Knight?

He continued to try to coax her in. "Just for five minutes. You said yourself no one could possibly know we're here. Why can't you just enjoy yourself?"

Now he was making her feel like a prude. A boring old stick-in-the-mud.

Which she was! When was the last time she'd enjoyed herself? Or gone out on a date that didn't involve work? When had she laughed, outside of these last few days with Donovan?

"I'd like to, but..."

"No more buts. Just dive in. I'll even turn around while you get undressed."

She stood for a few more seconds, considering it while Donovan continued to tread water with his back to her. Oh, what would it hurt? Five minutes. He was right. She'd done her job and done it well. No one could possibly find them here.

"All right," she said reluctantly, pulling her T-shirt off over her head. "But I'm not getting naked. I'm wearing undergarments that are perfectly respectable for swimming."

She was glad she'd worn the new black bra and matching panties that Doris had picked out for her, to go with the black dress. It almost looked like a real bikini.

He laughed. "Whatever floats your boat."

Shaking her head, Jocelyn stepped out of her shorts and folded everything neatly in a pile. She walked to the edge of the wharf.

"Okay, you can look now." She reached her arms

out in front of her, paused, then did a double forward flip through the air into the water.

As soon as she surfaced, she heard Donovan clapping and whooping. "That was amazing! What, you were an Olympic diver in your past life?"

She rubbed the water from her eyes. "No, but I was on a recreational swim team when I was a kid."

"You do everything well, don't you?" He swam closer.

She shrugged, trying not to think about the fact that he was completely naked in the water, not two feet away from her now, and she was in her underwear. If she moved any closer, she'd be able to touch him.

Lord, how she wanted to. Her body was practically humming with the desire to wrap her arms around his neck. To feel his cheek next to hers.

She wanted to let go of all her inhibitions—just this once—and do what Tess had suggested. Take advantage of this romantic summer night with the most handsome man on earth here beside her....

She took a deep breath and dunked her head, still trying to cool off, but realizing it was hopeless and she might as well resign herself to a painful, heated lust for the next half hour or so.

They dipped and dove and swam around each other as the sun disappeared behind the trees. The sensual feel of the water on Jocelyn's skin was sinfully erotic.

After a few minutes, Donovan came closer, treading water. "I have a goal," he said. "Concerning you."

She managed to keep her breathing steady as she

spoke. "What is it? You're not going to teach me to cook, are you?"

"No."

"To perform heart surgery on a raccoon?"

He laughed. "No."

"What then?"

Donovan's eyes smoldered with determination. "I want to make our time here pleasant for you."

As she gazed into his glimmering eyes, she couldn't think of a single thing to say. She wasn't quite sure what he was suggesting, though something about it made her feel warm inside.

Thankfully he elaborated. "The last two times you were here were some of the worst times in your life. This is a beautiful place, Jocelyn, and you should have happy memories of it. Feel as if those sadder times are over."

Beginning to understand his meaning, she slicked her wet hair back. "You mean you want to *cleanse* the cabin of its past for me?"

"In a matter of speaking, yes."

She was now treading water, very close to Donovan. "Why?"

He slowly blinked. "Because I want to see you smile."

"You've seen me smile."

"Not very often." The way he was looking at her now—with tenderness and caring—it was softening all her female powers of resistance. She didn't think she could keep herself from touching this incredibly charming man.

Yet it wasn't a sexual seduction that was going on here. He was just being inconceivably nice to her.

"What's this about?" she asked.

"It's about me wanting to make you happy."

She grinned at him. "That fortune cookie was right. You do like to fix things. It's why you want to open that grief counseling center to help children. It's why you became a heart surgeon. It's why you want to work on me now."

"I don't want to *work* on you."

"Yes, you do, but I'm not complaining. It's nice. No one's ever wanted to make me happy before. They always wanted to use me for their own happiness. But what about you, Donovan? You deserve joy in your life, too. Maybe I should have a goal as well."

They swam in circles around each other. "What are you suggesting?" His voice was a low murmur.

It was almost completely dark now. The moon was high in the sky, stars were sparkling. "I'm suggesting that if you feel the need to do something nice for me, I should do something nice for you in return."

"You already are. You're here, protecting me from a stalker."

"And you're paying me to do that, so we're even in that department."

"But if I try to make you happy while we're here…"

"Then I should do something similar for you."

Her heart was pounding against her ribs now. How far was she going to take this?

"And how do you intend to do that?"

She swam closer until she was nose-to-nose with him in the water. The magic of the night enveloped her; a brief shiver rippled through her body, followed by a juicy, delectable arousal between her legs.

She was tired of being the consummate professional, day in and day out, every minute of her life.

For once, she just wanted to be a woman.

"Like this." Then she slowly pressed her lips to
his.

Nine

The kiss was hot and wet and way overdue, Jocelyn thought, as she stroked her hands over Donovan's dripping hair and settled them on his shoulders. He folded her into his strong embrace, and in response, she let go of her reserve and wrapped her legs around him. His erection was already rock-hard, pressing against her, sending waves of wicked pleasure straight to her womanly center.

Before she knew what was happening, she was spinning slowly and deliciously through the water, then he was carrying her toward shore.

They emerged out of the water onto the beach, her legs still wrapped around his torso, his hands supporting her behind. Kissing deeply and passionately, they reached the blanket and Donovan sank with ease to his knees. He laid her on her back and came down smoothly on top of her.

Jocelyn opened her legs for him and tipped her head back and whimpered, while he kissed her neck and shoulders and heated her blood, and made her feel free and out of control. She could hardly believe this was happening—a beautiful, wet, naked man wanted her and was kissing her, outdoors beneath a star-speckled sky.

"Donovan, this is crazy," she whispered. "What if someone comes by?"

His discerning gaze scanned the yard around them. "I'll be listening."

All at once, she was on the other side of the fence, laying her safety and comfort in the hands of another person. It was peculiar to her, and infinitely wonderful.

Satisfied that he had eased her worries, Donovan pressed his lips to hers again and she swung eagerly into the pleasure he offered. He slid his hands down the side of her body, over the curve of her hips and back up to her breast, where he unhooked the front clasp of her bra, then began to stroke her. Tingling waves of delight moved through Jocelyn, followed by a sharp, intense ecstasy when he took her nipple into his mouth and brought her to the brink.

"Are you cold?" he whispered in her ear a few minutes later, his hot breath sending glorious little shivers down her spine.

"No, I'm burning up."

His gaze found hers and he smiled—warm, open and adoring. "Then I'll try to cool you down, though it won't be easy, love, considering I'm on fire, too."

He was still smiling when he kissed her again, and she cupped the strong muscles of his buttocks and pulled him tight against her. He continued to kiss and stroke her until she felt a surge of wild, impetuous lust. Her patience dissolved like sugar in liquid. She took his hand and guided it down, and like a skillful, insightful artist, he began to pleasure her with his finger.

She took him in her hand as well, and tried to give him the kind of pleasure he was giving her, but soon it was not enough and she wanted more. She wanted to feel him inside her. She was tired of holding back.

''Please tell me you have protection in your wallet,'' she said breathlessly.

''As a matter of fact, I do. I was hopeful about this.''

She smiled while he reached into the pocket of his balled up jeans, pulled out a condom and put it on.

Jocelyn wiggled out of her panties and slid them off. She sat up, gently pushed him onto his back on the blanket, and straddled him. ''I just want to make sure you know that this is me making you happy tonight, and not the other way around.''

He smiled wickedly, taking her hips in his big hands and shifting beneath her. ''Ah. You're trying to set this up so that I *owe* you.''

''Absolutely. And I'll expect payback as soon as you're able.'' She reached down to place him where she wanted him, then let her body glide down.

He filled her with a tantalizing completeness that sent her passions soaring.

His voice became breathless. ''Don't worry, it won't take me long to be able.''

He pushed her hair back from her face and pulled her down for another deep, soul-drenching kiss.

Their bodies moved in the moonlight, thrusting and withdrawing. Jocelyn's thoughts seemed to come to her on a floating cloud. How long had it been since she'd made love? Years. Not since Tom, and quite frankly, that had never been like this. Tonight she was overcome with rapture. She felt beautiful and erotic. Like a real woman. She felt cared for and protected, all of which was unfamiliar to Jocelyn, who was always on the other end of that spectrum.

This was pure bliss.

She plunged herself down and rubbed against him, again and again until a rushing flood of sensation overwhelmed them both. Jocelyn threw her head back and cried out; Donovan ground his hips forward, pushing into her with all his might. They climaxed simultaneously. It was the most incredible orgasm Jocelyn had ever experienced.

Weak and out of breath, she collapsed upon him. He held her for a few minutes, then rolled her over onto her back. She gazed up at him adoringly for a long, long time.

He leaned on one elbow looking down at her, caressing her face, playing with her hair. "What changed your mind about this?"

She took a moment to think about that. "It wasn't really a rational decision. If I was being rational, I wouldn't be here like this, naked and completely vulnerable on a beach with you. It was more of a surrender. I just couldn't fight it anymore."

"*It* being…?"

She ran her fingers through his hair. "The way I feel about you. The way you make me forget what I've somehow become, and make me remember that I'm a woman."

"You're *all* woman, Jocelyn. Even when you're pointing a gun at a stalker or speeding through the streets of Chicago. You turn a guy on. Don't ever forget it.''

She smiled up at him, wishing this moment could last forever, but knowing it couldn't. She had to go back to being on guard. She could not relax like this again. Or at least not without some preparatory safety precautions.

''Tell me,'' he said in a low, sexy voice, ''when would you like your services returned? I'm willing, and surprisingly enough, considering the brevity of our conversation just now, I'm quite able.''

Jocelyn laughed. ''*You* may be, but *I* need a break. My legs are like jelly!''

''Not to worry. You don't even have to move, just relax and stay on your back.''

She slapped his chest. ''You sound like you'd have me sleep through it.''

''Your comfort is my first priority. If you want to sleep, that would be fine.''

''While you're doing *that?*''

He laughed again. ''I'm joking Jocelyn. Why don't we go for another swim before we go inside?''

She gazed up at his warm, friendly eyes and felt relaxed. Safe. It was an unfamiliar sensation indeed. ''All right.''

He stood and helped her up. Jocelyn pointed down at her bra and undies on the grass. ''I guess I don't need those now.''

''Definitely not. Let's go.'' She took his hand, and laughing, they dashed naked across the dark beach and splashed with abandon into the lake.

Later that evening, after Donovan had a shower, he went downstairs to make popcorn. He could hear the shower still running in Jocelyn's bathroom, so he took his time getting things ready—lighting some candles, pouring their drinks, fluffing up the pillows on the blue chintz sofa.

She was taking a long time in the shower, he thought, as he opened the popcorn jar and went searching for cooking oil. He hoped she didn't regret what they'd done. He certainly didn't. In fact, he'd never been so ecstatic about making love to a woman before. Then again, he'd never known a woman like Jocelyn.

He found the oil and poured some into the heavy pot he'd set on the stove, then stood and stared down at it while he waited for it to heat up.

What was it about her that drove him so unbelievably wild? He wanted her, but more than just sexually. He wanted to be close to her—to get to know her and to reveal himself to her as well. He wanted to know everything about her childhood and her adulthood and her job and her personal life. He wanted to tell her about all his shortcomings and all his successes. Everything. He wanted her to know everything.

His insides stirred with an odd mixture of elation and fear. Was this love, or the beginnings of it?

Maybe it was, but how could he be sure? He'd never loved a woman before. He'd felt lust for them, yes, and been infatuated with girlfriends during high school and med school, but never had he loved any of them. He'd never felt a desire to enter into a commitment, or spend every waking minute of every day with them. He'd never felt connected to any of them, not like he did with Jocelyn. Perhaps it was her down-to-earth nature. She didn't put on any false airs. She was real, and he felt like he knew her as deeply as he knew his own soul.

An unfamiliar warmth moved through him, and he exhaled a deep sigh of tranquillity. It was one of the most pleasant sensations he'd ever experienced. He smiled.

A half a second later, something deep inside him warned him to be careful. He'd never given his heart to anyone before, and it wasn't so easy to let go of years of independence. There was also the fear that a relationship with Jocelyn might not work out. How the hell would he handle it if she disappeared from his life?

He'd been there before, to that devastating place.

In fact, he'd *always* been there. The sense of being alone was a part of his identity, even when he was with other people.

Except for Jocelyn.

A ripple of apprehension flowed through him. This was dangerous. In addition to his skepticism, she was still his bodyguard and he knew she wouldn't be ready or willing to shirk her responsibilities in order to become his full-time lover. She'd made it clear that she didn't like to get involved with clients, nor was she looking for a committed relationship. How many times had she told him that she didn't need anything in her life outside of her work?

Feeling suddenly nervous and uncertain about what was going on between them, he poured the popcorn kernels into the pot and covered it.

Jocelyn came out of her room a moment later, wearing a white terry cloth bathrobe and huge white socks that pooled around her ankles. She was rubbing a towel over her wet hair.

Donovan was mesmerized. "How is it possible you can look so good, just coming out of the shower?"

She gave him the bright, sparkling smile he'd been waiting to see. It almost knocked him backward into the pot.

Relief poured through him. He'd been worrying that she would feel awkward and uncomfortable when she came out, or be full of remorse. He'd been preparing himself for her to avoid meeting his gaze entirely.

"You're a charmer." She moved toward him and kissed him on the cheek. He wanted to laugh out loud with joy.

"What's cooking?" she asked.

"Popcorn."

She glanced at the pot. "You're making it on the stove? What a treat."

"*You're* the treat," he replied, enjoying the way she winked flirtatiously at him, then turned around and walked, hips swaying, into the living room.

He returned his attention to the stove and shook the pot continuously until a mouthwatering, movie-theater aroma filled the kitchen and the popcorn raised the lid right off the pot. He poured the popcorn into a bowl, then he melted butter to drizzle over the top.

Jocelyn was sitting on the sofa, twirling her hair around a finger, waiting for him. As soon as he set the bowl down on the coffee table, she pulled her legs up under her. "Donovan, we really have to talk about what happened between us tonight."

He was about to sit down, but found himself frozen on the spot. He couldn't move. "You asking me to politely back off is becoming a regular routine."

She took his hand. "I know, I'm sorry. Please sit down."

He gave in and did as she asked, though he would have preferred to go back to the way he'd felt five minutes ago when she'd given him that dazzling smile.

"Sounds like you did some thinking while you were in the shower."

He tried to fight the dread that was seeping into his gut, but it was worse this time. There was more at stake. The other times, his feelings for her hadn't had the chance to burrow too deeply inside him. He hadn't made love to her. He hadn't felt her warmth in his hands and in his heart. But now…he was too far over the edge.

"Yes, I did, and I think we need to set out some parameters."

"Parameters?"

Damn, he wasn't ready for the disappearing act yet. Despite his fears, he wanted more of her. He wanted to get inside her soul. He'd certainly come a long way toward that end, but as of now, there was still so much he didn't know about her. "I don't like the sound of that."

"I know, but it's important, considering the situation. I can't risk your safety."

He leaned forward and rested his elbows on his knees. "Look, I know you feel like you lost control down there at the lake, and I'm sorry if I pressured you into coming in, but you have to admit, what happened because of it was pretty great."

She squeezed his hand. "I'm not denying that at all. It was incredible, Donovan."

At least she was giving him that.

"We can manage this," he said. "You told me that we're safe here, that it's low-risk. The chances of anyone finding us are—"

She touched a finger to his lips to hush him. "You don't have to talk me into anything. I had a great time, too, and I want to do it again. I have every intention of it, actually."

His whole body flooded with relief, followed by heat and desire, in response to her blatantly sexual confession. "I beg your pardon?"

"I told you I'd done some thinking in the shower. I decided that because this is a low-risk detail at the moment, and since we've already broken the ice, so to speak, that we should set out some parameters to make sure that we can work it out. To make sure that we can make love again, and still exercise caution." She waved a hand toward the lake. "That was definitely *not* cautious."

"So, you're saying…"

"I'm saying I think we should stick to your bedroom from now on. With the door locked and the monitor on."

Donovan felt all the tension drain out of his shoulders like liquid. It was replaced by another type of tension—the kind that required a very satisfying cure.

He leaned back on the sofa and raked his fingers through his hair. "Thank God!"

Jocelyn laughed. "What, did you think I was going to torture you for the next few days? Torture both of us?"

He shook his head. "I don't know what I thought. I was afraid of that, I guess."

She swayed toward him and took his face in her hands. "What happened down at the lake was amazing, Donovan. I have no regrets. We're here in this great spot, I'm attracted to you and you seem to be attracted to me. We're both adults, so I don't see why we shouldn't enjoy each other, as long as we act responsibly and take precautions."

She was making it sound like a casual, temporary fling.

A part of him wanted to talk her out of that—to convince her that they could be so much more than that, if they tried.

But in light of the uncertainty he still felt about how willing he was to risk his own heart, he decided it would be best to just nod and say yes. She was offering a few days of no-strings-attached lovemaking. Maybe it was all she could give. For all he knew, maybe it was all *he* could give. He couldn't possibly predict, because this was uncharted territory.

This was a good thing, he decided, smiling at her and leaning in for a kiss. It would give them both time to get to know each other, without ever really committing to anything more. Then, if it didn't work out, it wouldn't be too serious.

At least, he didn't think it would be. Considering the way he felt at the moment—all hot and bothered and emotionally exhilarated—there might not be any way to prevent it from becoming serious.

Jocelyn raked her fingers through his hair and kissed him deeply, distracting him from his thoughts. Heady temptations seared his brain.

He tried to ease her back onto the sofa, but she

rested her hands on his chest. "Remember what I said."

"Precautions?"

"Yes. So why don't we take that popcorn upstairs and eat it later?"

He smiled down at her and kissed her one more time. "I like the way you think."

She raised a flirty eyebrow and got up, taking him by the hand and leading him to the stairs.

He would just have to be patient, he decided, and see where the next few days would take them....

"You know, I was actually surprised that you hired me," Jocelyn said the next morning as she pulled the drapes open across the huge windows.

Donovan leaned up in bed on one elbow, the white sheet slung across his waist. "Why?"

"Because I'm a woman."

Jocelyn gazed down at the awesome sight of his handsome face and muscular, sun-bronzed chest, and felt her insides melt, but she fought the urge to get back in bed and make love with him, because they'd already made love twice that morning, and they needed breakfast.

"You had a great reputation," he said.

She went to get her bathrobe, on the floor by the door. "Yes, but I didn't think you considered me a real bodyguard. Part of me thought you just wanted me to come and stay in your penthouse because you thought I was cute and it would be fun."

He smiled, looking taken aback. "It *was* fun."

She picked up one of his socks on the floor and flung it at him.

"Seriously," he said, "I did need a new alarm

system, and for some reason I trusted you to provide the security I needed.''

''But would you have given in so easily to Mark and hired me if I had been a short, bald man?''

He gazed at her for a moment. ''What's with the questions?''

She pulled on her robe, tied it around her waist, and shrugged.

He pointed at her. ''You just want to know if I'm still the playboy that you thought I was when you first met me, and if you're my most recent diversion.''

Jocelyn combed her fingers through her hair, wishing he wasn't always so perceptive where her emotions were concerned. Even though she'd come to realize he wasn't at all shallow, she was still afraid of something. She wasn't quite sure what it was yet. ''You can't blame me. I suppose I want to understand what's going on between us.''

His chest heaved with a sigh. ''I thought last night you said this was just about enjoying each other while we're here.''

Was that really all he wanted? she wondered, surprised at how hurt she felt by his reminder. She should have asked him what his intentions were at that moment, but she couldn't. A question like that would be too needy and demanding, and he was right, she *had* said they would just enjoy each other. She'd offered him a few nights of pleasure, nothing more—it was what she'd wanted herself—and she had no right to change her mind now.

Was she changing her mind? The thought terrified her. Everything had been so wonderful last night down at the lake, and through the night in his bed.

Donovan had not only given her more pleasure than she'd ever dreamed possible, he'd been gentle and caring and loving.

It was all so new. So overwhelming. She didn't know what to make of it.

"Hey, I'm sorry," she said, trying to hide the depth of her unbidden fears. "I shouldn't have brought it up."

"Brought what up, exactly?"

A flurry of panic coursed through her. He was staring at her intently. Watching her. Wanting to know what she was getting at.

Oh God, was she scaring him off?

She was scaring herself.

"The fact that you hired me," she replied, skirting the *real* question, for him as well as for herself. She needed time to sort out her feelings. "Some people don't trust a woman to do the job. Come on, let's go get some breakfast."

He tossed the sheet off and got out of bed, then fished through his suitcase for a pair of shorts. He pulled them on and followed her down the stairs.

"I hired you because I trusted you," he said. "You have a competent air about you."

Jocelyn entered the kitchen. "Thank you. Why don't I cook breakfast this morning?"

"All right." He sat down on one of the stools at the counter, while she pulled eggs and bacon out of the fridge and set to work. She laid the bacon slices in a skillet to fry.

"So tell me," he said, "why did you leave the Secret Service?"

"To be honest, for the money." She cracked some

eggs into a bowl and began to beat them with a whisk.

"That's surprising. I thought you hated that kind of thing."

"I hate people attaching more value to their cars and boats than to their loved ones. I don't hate money. In fact, I appreciate it very much when I can put it to good use. I'm sending my younger sister to Juliard."

He perked up at that. "You never mentioned that before."

"It never came up."

"Do you have any other brothers or sisters?"

"No, just Marie. She's eighteen and a very talented cello player. She moved in with my aunt after my mom died and no one could afford to send her to a good music school, so I went out on my own to try to cover the expense. Besides that, I like the independence of running my own business."

"Are you musical, too?"

She smiled and poured the eggs into the frying pan she'd set on the stove. "I like to sing."

"You are full of surprises. Sing something."

"Not while I'm cooking! I need to concentrate."

"Oh, yeah, I forgot. Cooking is one of the things you *don't* do. But it looks to me like you're doing it pretty well."

She gave him a look over her shoulder. "I didn't say I *couldn't* do it. I just said I didn't like to."

He rose from the stool to come around the counter and approach her from behind. "Seems to me, you're good at everything. This especially…"

He slid his hands around her waist and nibbled her

neck, while she stirred the eggs on the stove. Goose bumps erupted and tickled all over her body.

"You're distracting me. I'm going to burn the eggs."

She felt his erection pressing against her bottom. Desire coursed through her. Incapable of resisting the heated power of it, she set down her spatula and turned around to kiss him. She wrapped her arms around his neck and reveled in the feel of his wet, open mouth and his tongue mingling with hers. How was it possible a man could press all her buttons with such unbelievable intensity?

After a moment or two, the bacon snapped and sizzled in the skillet, reminding her that she was in charge of breakfast. She smiled and pushed him away. "We can't do this constantly, Donovan. We're human. We need to eat."

He kissed her on the cheek and returned to the stool. "Being a doctor, you'd think I'd remember that."

While Jocelyn cooked breakfast, they talked more about her sister, Marie, then about Donovan's plans with the grief counseling center.

They sat down to eat, discussing what would happen after the police caught Cohen, and how involved Donovan would be in the legal proceedings.

After breakfast, Donovan rose from the table and picked up both their plates. Jocelyn made a move to rise.

"No, you stay here and enjoy your coffee," he said. "I'll get this."

He's a dream, she thought, thanking him with a kiss. Still in her bathrobe, she pushed the sliding door open, then stepped out onto the deck to enjoy the view of the lake. She sat down on a lounge chair and sipped her coffee, remembering how incredible Donovan had been in bed the night before, how he had brought her to tears when she'd climaxed. Tears of joy. Tears of hope.

God, she was losing control. He may be a dream, she told herself, but he's still your client. A client who has never had, with any woman, a relationship that lasted.

She shifted uneasily in her chair. What in the world was she doing? She was a professional, and she'd broken the cardinal rule: Never get emotionally involved.

Yet here she was, happier than she'd ever been in her entire life, wanting to touch Donovan and feel his arms around her, wanting to talk to him and fill whatever void still existed in his heart from losing his parents. She wanted to help him find true happiness and show him how wonderful a lasting love could be....

Her mind suddenly clouded with self-doubt. Lasting love? What did she know of that? She'd been single for years since Tom left her. She still carried around anger at her father for leaving her mother. What did she know of the kind of happiness that came with lifelong love? Nothing.

A fine pair they made.

Jocelyn heard the sound of pots clanging in the kitchen, and took another sip of her coffee.

Yes, she cared deeply for Donovan, maybe she was even falling in love with him, but was she brave enough to throw all caution to the wind, and jump in headfirst? She wasn't sure.

All she knew was that for now, she had to keep

her feet on the ground and remember that this was a week of pleasure, nothing more. She didn't think she had what it took to lead Donovan out of the lonely place he'd known all his life, and he most likely didn't have what it took to keep a relationship going—even though it was no fault of his own.

Together, they were probably ill-fated. She would do well to remember that.

Ten

Over the next three days, when they weren't making love in a locked bedroom, Jocelyn and Donovan went fishing, swimming and hiking in the woods. The owners of the cabin delivered live lobsters one night, which Donovan cooked for supper with melted butter and Italian bread. The other evenings, Donovan barbecued, and afterward, they went skinny-dipping in the moonlight.

It was the most romantic few days Jocelyn had ever known in her life—and the most confusing, because everything was perfect. Donovan was affectionate, attentive and a generous lover. He cooked for her, rubbed her shoulders and listened to whatever she wanted to talk about.

She couldn't imagine that life could be like this every day—that this wasn't some special dream world. There had to be a hitch. There always was.

"Tell me something," Donovan said in bed one night, after they'd made love. "When you were trying to convince me not to buy that black dress for you, you said you could guarantee it was something you'd never wear again. Why? And why do you always wear that plain brown suit and flat shoes, when you'd look terrific in something…else?"

Jocelyn sat up and smiled. "That's a tactful way of telling me I dress like crap."

He laughed. "You know that's not what I mean. You just seem to want to play *down* your looks."

Jocelyn lay back down, resting her cheek on Donovan's shoulder. "I guess I've never been able to stop fighting what I always had to fight as a child."

"What was that?"

"My father's wayward sense of what was important. He wasn't the warmest individual on the planet, and the only time I ever got a smile or a compliment from him was when I was dressed up like a little doll. He couldn't stand to see me in jeans, or dirty from playing outside, and he was completely unattracted to my mother when she was wearing her terry cloth bathrobe around the house. Then, when he left, he told her it was because she didn't care enough about her appearance. He took off with a younger woman who wore short skirts, glittery earrings and lots of hairspray. I'll never forget what she looked like, and my poor mother, who was the kindest, most loving person in the world, never got over that. She became insecure and self-conscious, even when I tried to tell her every day that she was the most beautiful woman in the world to me. I guess I just don't ever want people to like me because I *look* good. I can't stand the superficiality of that."

Jocelyn couldn't believe she had just told Donovan all of that. She'd never told anyone those things, except her assistant, Tess, and that had been after two years of working together.

He rubbed a thumb over her shoulder. "It doesn't matter what you wear, Jocelyn, you *always* look good."

She kissed his bare chest. "But you're not shallow, Donovan. Lots of people are, and I don't want or need to dress up to impress *them*."

"But by trying to look like one thing—a tough, untouchable bodyguard—you're doing the same thing your father was doing, only the opposite way. You're still putting a lot of emphasis on your appearance, trying to give off a certain impression, when it doesn't matter. You can wear short skirts if you want to, and you'll still be the same person. You'll still be smart and funny and tough."

She sighed. "That's a unique way to look at it."

"Maybe. I just wonder if the real reason you've always played down your looks was to keep people away, because you said yourself that you don't believe in happily ever after." He kissed her forehead, brushing her hair back with his lips. "Jocelyn, I don't want to be one of those people you try to push away."

She leaned up on one elbow to look him in the eye. "You're trying to fix me, aren't you?"

His expression was open, friendly, adoring. "I just want you to know that you could wear *anything* in front of me—fancy or plain—and you'd still be extraordinary. And I'm sorry that your father couldn't love you for the person you were on the inside. He was very wrong to take his family for granted. He had no idea how lucky he was to have you both. Maybe someday he'll realize it."

She rested her head on his chest again. "How did you get to be so optimistic?"

"I don't know, maybe it's because of the ideals I have about my parents and the things I remember about them. My grandmother told me they were like two peas in a pod. They had everything in common and cherished each other, and when they had me, they grew even closer. We were a tight unit, the three of us, and nothing was more important to them than our little family—not their jobs, not their money, not their belongings. Gram told me they were soul mates."

"That's beautiful, Donovan. You were lucky to grow up with a promising outlook on relationships."

He gazed down at her. "Why do I get the feeling you think I'm being unrealistic?"

She shook her head defensively. "I don't. All I know is what I've seen in my life. Maybe the kind of happiness your parents knew is possible for some people."

"But not you?"

She looked at his face, contemplating what she believed. What she thought was possible. Until now, she'd been a skeptic, but Donovan was touching something inside of her. She was dreaming of happiness now, imagining a beautiful future with him even though she was scared to death that she was setting herself up for disappointment.

Still, she'd never been inclined to dream of a perfect future before, and that said something. Donovan had given her hope. "I...I guess I would like to believe that maybe it is possible."

His face warmed at her words—words that signified a lowering of her shield. Words that gave him hope, too.

"You're beautiful." He gathered her into his arms and pressed his mouth hotly to hers. Jocelyn let all her worries go, and gave herself over completely to the pleasure of his lovemaking, which tonight was like a wonderful, erotic dream.

She would worry about reality tomorrow.

"Want to go upstairs and play Monopoly?" Donovan asked, after supper when it looked like it was going to rain.

Jocelyn smiled at him. "Monopoly…is that some fancy term for the horizontal mambo?"

He laughed. "No, I think the fancy term for 'the horizontal mambo' is 'the horizontal mambo.' I mean play real Monopoly."

"Why upstairs?" she asked suspiciously.

"I thought we could play it on the bed, in the nude."

Oh, he was delicious. She sauntered up close to him and slid a hand down his pants. "It's only fair to warn you, I used to be addicted to Monopoly when I was a kid. You don't know what you're getting into."

He took a deep breath but didn't let it out. "I think you're the one who's getting into something dangerous at the moment. If you're not careful, we'll never even get near the game."

Jocelyn slowly removed her hand from Donovan's jeans, and backed away toward the stairs. "And which game would that be?" Then she started to run. Donovan chased her.

They bounded up the stairs, laughing and hooting. Donovan caught up just as she neared the bed. He leaped on top of her and flipped her over onto the soft mattress, coming down, kissing her mouth and pressing his pelvis into hers.

"Let's play Monopoly later," Jocelyn whispered, her body tingling with sweet, lusty sensations.

They both rose up on their knees on the bed to take off their T-shirts, still kissing whenever possible. Within seconds, they were out of their jeans and falling back onto the bed.

"Wait!" Jocelyn said. "We didn't lock the door."

"I'll get it." Donovan scrambled off the bed. He flicked the lock and turned on the monitor, then turned to where she lay, naked on top of the covers.

Completely overwhelmed by the loving expression on her face, he stopped at the foot of the bed to gaze down at her, then rested his open palm on his chest. He spoke softly. "You are so beautiful."

Donovan's heart was aching. Aching! He couldn't take his eyes off Jocelyn. She was a tiny piece of heaven, there on the bed, waiting for him, her eyes honest and adoring. How could he ever walk away from this?

He gently came down upon her slender body and held her in his arms.

He felt joyful, more complete somehow as his lips brushed hers and her body melted perfectly into his. They were made for each other, and he was completely in her power, overcome by the compulsion to hold her tighter and closer, to make love to her tonight and every night until the end of their days.

His blood quickened in his veins at the frightening decision—that he wanted her forever.

The absolute certainty was strange and foreign, and so potent that he felt it like a blazing inferno inside his chest. He didn't want to ever let her go.

She wrapped her long, beautiful legs around him and kissed his neck, ran her hands up and down his spine, and he squeezed her tight against him. Soon, she was inching down the bed and taking him in her mouth, bringing him to the brink of insanity. He couldn't take it. It was so good....

"Jocelyn," he whispered, running his hands through her hair. "I've never felt like this. Come here." He pulled her up beside him and reached into the drawer for a condom. He put it on, then he rolled on top of her, and with a swift, urgent need, he entered her in a single thrust.

She whimpered amorously. "I've never felt like this, either, Donovan."

He made love to her in the twilight, slowly. Very slowly, with deliberate attention to what she was feeling, intensifying the things she liked, rising up on his forearms and using his legs and hips to build the pleasure.

She moved with him in harmony on the bed. Sexually, he had come to know her very well these past few days. He knew what stirred her into that whirlwind of excitement, and what sent her soaring. He knew how to move inside her, how to work the friction—when to ease it, when to build it.

He took his time delivering the pleasure tonight. He spent each passing heartbeat watching her face and giving her all that he had. He wanted to give her everything, and he wanted this to last.

She opened her eyes and gazed up at him lazily, then cupped his face in her soft hands. They watched each other moving in the dim light. Time seemed to stand still. Donovan's heart swelled with love.

Yes, it was love.

"Jocelyn." He was approaching that place…the burning eruption. His mind began to spin. He lowered his body to hers and held her tightly in his arms, recognizing the signs. She was approaching that place, too. "I don't want this to end."

He didn't just mean their lovemaking. He meant all of it.

Then he quickened the rhythm, bringing her with him to the edge of desire, then over the edge to the beyond where all their needs were sated, and euphoria enveloped them completely.

It was different this time. The deepest places in his heart were involved and committed.

He held her tightly afterward, squeezing her close, wishing he could get even closer. "Jocelyn."

For a long time they lay in each other's arms until the twilight turned to darkness and rain began to tap on the skylight over their heads. Seconds later, it intensified to a torrential downpour, drumming noisily on the glass.

Jocelyn snuggled in closer. "Guess we won't be stargazing tonight."

Donovan kissed her forehead. "I like the sound of the rain. It reminds me of camping with my grandmother in her trailer when I was a kid. We always had the worst luck with weather, but it was nice all the same. Cozy."

"My parents took me tenting when I was really little, but only a few times. We weren't much into family vacations, then when Dad left, we didn't do much other than the usual routine. I'd love to go to a campground someday.''

"Let's do it," Donovan said.

"Yeah, sure."

He tipped her face up to see her eyes, but he couldn't see the expression in the darkness. "No, I really mean it. Let's go as soon as they catch Cohen. As soon as he's behind bars. We'll bring a bottle of champagne."

She nodded, but he sensed a sadness in her.

"What's wrong?" he asked,

"Nothing."

He sat up. "No, something's wrong. You seem down."

"It's nothing, Donovan."

"It is something. Tell me what's the matter."

For a long moment, she lay in silence, then she sat up, too. "Reality is settling in."

"What do you mean?"

"I mean, we're going to have to leave this place eventually, and I've been having such a great time."

"So have I, but we can have a great time in Chicago, too."

She shrugged. "I just think that when we go back to our real lives, this will seem like a dream."

He leaned away from her to flick on the light. They both squinted as their eyes adjusted. "Didn't you hear what I said before? That I didn't want this to end?"

"I thought you were talking about—" she waved her hand over the bed "—this."

He shook his head. "No, I was talking about *all* of it with you. I want to keep seeing you, Jocelyn."

She swiveled to put her feet on the floor so that

he was looking at her bare back. "I'm not sure that would be a good idea."

His heart wrenched painfully in his chest. Was this the disappearing act? No, that couldn't be....

He was sure she cared for him. He couldn't have mistaken the way she touched him, the way she looked at him and spoke to him. They'd talked about so many personal things over the past few days. They'd opened up to each other. They'd made love.

"Why not?" he asked. "We're great together, and once you're no longer my bodyguard, there won't be any reason to resist this."

"There's a big reason."

He swallowed hard over the sickening lump of dread in his throat. "Is there something you haven't told me?"

She turned slightly on the bed to look at him. "No, it's nothing like that. It's what I've told you before—that I don't believe in happily ever after." She must have seen the expression of shock and hurt on his face, because she reached for his hand. "It's not that I don't trust you or care for you. It's that I don't trust myself not to fall so hard for you that I would never be able to recover from it when it ended."

"What makes you so sure it would end?"

"It always ends."

"That's not true. Lots of people spend their whole lives together."

"Not people like you and me."

Donovan couldn't speak for a moment. He raked a hand through his hair. "Jocelyn, I felt that way, too. Maybe I still do a little. I can't see into the future, and hell, I'm as scared as you are about how this might turn out, but I've never felt this way about anyone before. This is different. So if the circumstances are different, maybe we can be different, too.''

She shook her head. ''I don't know, Donovan. My parents were in love once, and look what happened to them. My dad left my mom for a younger, prettier woman and never looked back. My mom was devastated, because she really, really loved him. She never got over it. She was still crying years later when she looked at his picture. It was heartbreaking for me to see, and I don't want to go through that. I don't want to be like her someday.''

''So you're going to pass up on what we have together, because there's a *chance* it might not work out? Jocelyn, you might be missing out on a happiness that could last forever.''

''I'm not a risk taker. I do what it takes to prevent dangerous things from happening.''

''That's a fine philosophy for your work, but not for your life. If you don't risk the bad, you'll never experience the really great stuff. I've been alone my whole life, and you're the first person I've ever felt close to. I can't let you disappear. I need you.''

She turned her back on him again. ''You're just feeling this way because of the situation. You're feeling vulnerable, and I make you feel safe. What you feel isn't permanent, Donovan. When Cohen is caught, you won't need me.''

''I will need you, and it has nothing to do with Cohen. Don't you trust me? Don't you believe that I care for you deeply, and that I want you? Hell, Jocelyn, I'm in love with you.''

She turned to look at him, her face pale with astonishment. She sat motionless, staring at him.

"I love you," he repeated, sliding closer and pushing a lock of hair away from her face. "I've never said that to anyone before. Doesn't that count for anything?"

"Tom said those words to me, too, and my father said them to my mother."

"I'm not Tom or your father. I'm Donovan Knight, the man who loves you and wants to spend his life with you."

Jocelyn got off the bed like it had caught fire. "What are you saying?"

"I'm saying I want you to marry me. Marry me, Jocelyn."

Her eyes grew wide like saucers. She grabbed her head in her hands and paced to the door. "This is too sudden! You're not being sensible. We hardly know each other."

He tried to follow her. "That's not true. We know each other better than some people can know each other in a lifetime. We click."

Her face winced. She looked like she was going to cry. "Please don't do this, Donovan. You're pulling me in."

"That's my intention."

"But I don't want to be pulled in! I want to stay safe and be in control, at least until I can feel more sure of things."

"Love is not a security assignment, Jocelyn. There will never be guarantees."

"That's what scares me."

"But if it works out, think of how great it will be."

"*If* it works out? I can't hang my hopes or my future happiness on anything that begins with the word *if*." She reached for her clothes and pulled her T-shirt over her head. "I'm sorry, Donovan, I need to be alone for a while. I'll be in my room."

With that, she walked out.

What just happened? Jocelyn wondered frantically as she shut her bedroom door and leaned against it. How had a simple week of pleasure gotten so out of control? And who started the heavy ball rolling? Had she encouraged Donovan subconsciously somehow? Maybe she had been dreaming a little too much about happily ever after, and she'd communicated that to him.

Or was he right? Did they click like they'd never clicked with anyone else in their lives? Was this the once-in-a-lifetime fairy tale?

Jocelyn dropped her forehead into the heels of her hands and padded to the bed. If only she had more experience with this sort of thing. She'd shied away from dating ever since things went sour with Tom, and she was way out of her league here. For all she knew, maybe all infatuations felt like this at first—a burning fire that refused to be extinguished. Maybe it was just lust. Maybe it would pass for both of them as soon as they got home.

Or maybe it wouldn't.

She lay down on the bed she hadn't slept on since they'd arrived. What was she going to do?

Her cell phone rang in the kitchen, and she jumped. Jocelyn hurried out of her room to answer it. "Hello?"

"Jocelyn, it's Tess. How's everything going?"

Jocelyn contemplated how she should answer that question. "Oh, you know, everything's fine."

"Yeah? You've been having a good time?"

Jocelyn recognized Tess's playful, prying tone, but she wasn't about to give her the dirty details when she didn't even understand them herself. Tess probably wouldn't even believe it if she told her. *Yes, I've been having a wonderful time, and Prince Charming just proposed marriage....*

"What's up?" Jocelyn asked.

Thankfully, Tess stuck to business. "I have news. The police picked up Ben Cohen this afternoon. He's in custody and he confessed to everything."

"You're kidding me." Jocelyn sank into a chair at the table. "That didn't take long."

"Yeah, it's great, isn't it? You can come home anytime. Oh, and I tentatively booked you on a new assignment. An animal rights activist has been getting threatening letters."

Feeling numb all of the sudden, Jocelyn sat and watched the rain slide down the windows in fast-moving rivulets. It was over. They'd caught Cohen. It was time to go home.

"Jocelyn? Are you there?"

She snapped herself back to reality. "Yeah, Tess, I'm here. That's great. Uh...we'll pack up and leave tonight. I'm sure the police will want to speak to Donovan first thing in the morning."

"Yes, they did ask about that." There was a long silence on the other end of the line. "So what do you want me to do about the animal rights activist? Do you want to take that assignment? She's pretty anxious."

Jocelyn continued to stare at the rain-covered window. Lightning flashed somewhere in the distance.

Her heart throbbed a few times in her chest, then she took a deep breath and stood up.

"Yes. Take it, and tell her I'll start immediately. I'll do the advance work tomorrow."

She flipped her phone closed, and turned around. Donovan was standing at the bottom of the stairs, staring at her, his brows drawn together with anguish and disbelief.

Jocelyn's stomach flared with nervous knots. "I didn't realize you were listening."

His voice was low and controlled. "I can see that." He slowly strode toward her. "What's going on, Jocelyn? And why do I get the feeling that if you have it your way, after tonight I'm never going to see you again?"

Eleven

Jocelyn strode to her room to pack her things. "It won't be like that. We've gotten close, Donovan. We can keep in touch."

He followed and stood in her doorway. "The old 'we'll still be friends' routine? Come on, Jocelyn."

She opened dresser drawers and pulled out her clothes, balling them up and tossing them into her suitcase.

Donovan strode to her and took her arm. "Stop packing for a second and talk to me."

"We can talk in the car. I want to get going because it's a long drive and I want to get you back to your penthouse by midnight."

"You're just gonna drop me off and keep going?"

She paused for a moment to gaze into his eyes. "There's no more danger. Cohen is behind bars, and there's no point in you being charged my fees for another day.''

"Oh, so you're doing me a favor, is that it? Saving me a few dollars? I didn't realize I was paying for your services at *night*.''

Jocelyn's mouth fell open. She supposed she deserved that, for all the pain she was inflicting upon him. All because she was afraid to take a risk.

Feeling defeated, she sat down on the edge of the bed. "Donovan, I'm sorry about this. I know I'm being a jerk.'' He stood a few feet away, listening. She gazed up at him imploringly. "Maybe we could see each other but take it slow. Cool our jets and just try to bring it back a notch.''

He considered that a moment, then shook his head, his expression grim. "I don't think I can do that. It would be hell for me. It would be like trying to swim upstream in whitewater rapids. I'm in love with you, Jocelyn. Passionately. I don't want to be away from you. I want to come home to you every night and wake up with you every morning. Life's too short to do it any other way.''

Jocelyn sighed heavily and stared down at the white T-shirt she was squeezing into a ball on her lap. "I can't be that person, Donovan. I can't be your doting wife, who gives all of her heart to you. It would never be real. I would always be holding back and you'd know it. You deserve better. You *need* something better, because you've never had it, and I can see how much you want it. Believing that I'm the one for you…it's just wishful thinking. You're in love with the person I was here, but this isn't the real me, and frankly, it's not the real you, either. We were pretending. Pretending that life was perfect and nothing could touch us. It won't be like that when we go back.''

For a long time, he stared at her in the lamplight, then he nodded and began to back away. ''All right. I'll go pack my things.''

He left the room. Jocelyn was shocked. Shocked by everything she had just said, and shocked that he was gone.

She continued to sit on the bed, staring after him in silence. Her eyes filled with hot, stinging tears. Her insides were churning.

She hated hurting him like this! But wasn't it better to do it now, when it was just an infatuation, before things got truly serious?

A tear trickled down her cheek and she wiped it away. God, when was the last time she'd cried? She couldn't remember. She'd spent her whole life trying to be tough, pushing pain away. She'd never cried when Tom left her, or when her father left. Anger and resentment had smothered any possibility of tears.

Looking back on it, she supposed she had never truly felt that Tom's heart was involved—or her father's, either. They'd been callous men, more concerned with appearances and what the neighbors thought than what she or anyone else was feeling.

Donovan was the opposite. He felt everything deeply, which was why he was working on a grief center for kids, because his heart was still enduring the hole left behind when his parents drove over that cliff and perished in front of his eyes. It was why he was still single. He was not cavalier about love.

Yet she had been savage toward his tender heart. What did that make her? How could she have done that? Was she really the cold, tough, unfeeling person she pretended to be? In not wanting to be like her mother, had she become like her father?

Her chest throbbed with a painful, squeezing agony. She didn't feel like her father on the inside. She felt more like a wounded bird, who couldn't manage to find her wings.

Yet she had found them briefly these past few days with Donovan, when she'd clutched at him and cried out his name in the darkness, or when she'd laughed with him or told him secrets about her childhood.

Was it too late for her to find her wings? Too late to believe in a love that could last forever?

She gazed up at the ceiling and heard Donovan slamming things around upstairs. She didn't know. She just didn't know.

After a long, silent drive back to Chicago in the pouring rain and darkness, Jocelyn escorted Donovan up to his penthouse. She did a thorough search to make sure everything was okay, then stood in his marble vestibule, preparing to say goodbye.

"So this is it," Donovan said flatly.

She flinched at his icy tone. "Donovan, I'm sorry. I've accepted another assignment and—"

"You don't have to explain. You already did that at the cabin."

They stared at each other for a few seconds, then Donovan stuck out his hand. "It was a pleasure working with you. If you need references, I'd be happy to give them. You did an excellent job with the security."

Feeling numb and confused, Jocelyn gazed up at

his beautiful face, listened to his detached tone, and shook his hand. "Donovan…"

She didn't know what to say! She wasn't any good at this. She'd never been in this situation before, and she'd spent half her life struggling to keep people at a distance. He was doing the same thing to her now, and it was killing her inside.

Rising up on her toes, she leaned toward him and kissed him on the cheek. "I had a great time with you. I'll never forget it."

"Neither will I." His voice told her he was shaken by the kiss. So was she.

"I should go. It's late and we both need to catch up on some sleep."

Donovan nodded.

She walked to the elevator and pressed the down button. With her back to him, she listened for his door closing, but it didn't. He was still standing there, watching her. Her stomach tightened into knots, her heart racing.

Something was tugging at her. Telling her to turn around and dash into his arms, kiss him and tell him how sorry she was. Tell him that she loved him and never wanted to let him go.

But her brain wouldn't let her. What about tomorrow, she heard herself asking, and the day after that? She couldn't make important decisions like this on a heart-splitting impulse. She had to think about the ramifications of her actions. She needed time….

The elevator dinged and the brass doors opened smoothly. She stepped inside.

She didn't want to turn around. She couldn't look at his face one more time, because she might change her mind. Yet she had to turn around to press the lobby button.

Jocelyn took a deep breath and faced the front. Whatever she was afraid of was a nonissue. Donovan's door was just clicking shut.

"I can't believe you got on that elevator," Tess said from her desk, tearing the paper off the bottom of her blueberry muffin. "Prince Charming wants to marry you, and you walk away."

Back in the familiar feel of her brown pantsuit, Jocelyn stood at the filing cabinet in the reception area of her office, looking for something in the top drawer. "Life isn't a fairy tale. It all happened too fast. People can't make important decisions like that based on a few romantic days with their bodyguard at a lakeside retreat, when their life's in danger."

"*He* did."

She threw Tess an impatient glare. "That doesn't make it sensible. He would have regretted it. I did him a favor last night. He'll realize that as soon as he gets back into his regular routine. I give each of us three days tops to forget about this. Where's the file on limo services?"

"How can you be so sure? And what about *you?* Did you do *yourself* a favor last night, turning down a marriage proposal to the most handsome man alive, who also happens to be a rich doctor and great in bed?"

Jocelyn held up a hand. "Don't go there. I don't want to think about that."

"Why not? If you don't think about it, you're not facing it and you'll be living in a bubble, out of touch with reality."

"Tess, I don't want to—"

The phone rang. Tess picked it up. "Mackenzie Security."

Her gaze lifted and she started pointing frantically at the phone, mouthing the words, *It's him!*

There could have been a power surge in Jocelyn's veins. She stood at the filing cabinet, panic filling every corner of her being, while she watched Tess and waited for her to say something.

Tess kept her gaze down, nodding and saying, "Certainly," in that professional tone she had down. A few seconds later, she hung up the phone and Jocelyn's heart broke into a thousand pieces.

"What did he want?"

Tess grimaced. "He wants me to fax him the bill instead of mailing it, so he can drop his check off today."

A lump the size of a grapefruit was forming in Jocelyn's throat. She couldn't talk.

"Maybe he wants to see you, and can't wait," Tess offered helpfully.

Jocelyn knew better. She shook her head and went back to what she was doing. Her fingers crawled over the tops of her files. "I don't think so. He wants to put a tidy finish on things."

"Maybe not. Maybe he'll show up with flowers."

Jaded as she was, Jocelyn sighed and shook her head again, fighting off the tiny fragment of hope that, despite her attempts to crush it, still lived inside her.

That tenacious little hope languished, however, later in the day, when a check arrived by courier.

* * *

Jocelyn had given herself three days to get over Donovan.

Three weeks had gone by.

After finishing her assignment with the animal rights activist, she sat in her apartment eating Cheerios and watching television at ten o'clock at night. She had no work lined up for tomorrow. She'd told Tess to give her a few days off. She'd never needed time off before, but she'd never felt tired before, either.

Tired. Lord, she just wanted to crawl into her bed and lie there for a week. Everything had gotten so...busy. There was nothing to smile about. The animal rights activist treated her like she was invisible—which was nothing new. She expected and even encouraged that from her principals. But since her week with Donovan, she'd come to realize that being invisible wasn't all it was cracked up to be. Sure it was okay on the job, but what about outside of her work? Who was she?

With Donovan, she had felt alive. She'd felt like a woman. Someone with an identity, even though she was away from everything that was a part of who she was—her apartment, her car, her office. Donovan had made her feel like she mattered in the world, even when she was naked, swimming in the lake.

What she'd had with him was the least materialistic thing she'd ever known. Yet it was the most real.

And she had walked away from it! Worse than walked away. She'd hurt him in the process, when he'd been hurt far too much in his life.

Would he ever forgive her? she wondered, longing for the bliss and tranquillity she'd felt in his arms day after day when she had been in his employ. She had thought it would fade away by now, but the hurt was only getting worse. She missed him. God, how she missed him. What a coward she had been.

She rose from the sofa to put her empty bowl in the dishwasher, then poured soap in and pressed the start button. She went to her bedroom and gazed at her empty bed, then at her treadmill and free weights, thought about what she did for a living, all the dangerous situations she'd been in. Wasn't she supposed to be tough and strong? What had happened to her? Where was her grit?

A vision of Donovan's beautiful face appeared in her mind, along with the memory of his kindness and tender generosity. Three weeks had gone by and she was nowhere near to being over him.

This was not just a fleeting infatuation.

A new sense of purpose filled her. She went to her closet and began rifling through her clothes, looking for something feminine to wear. She'd had three weeks to think about Donovan, and in her heart and soul she finally knew that this was not an impulse.

Tomorrow, she was going to see Donovan again, and come hell or high water, she was going to rise above her fears. For the first time in her life, she was going to take a risk with her personal life. How it would turn out, she had no idea. She would just have to have faith.

Jocelyn was getting out of the shower when her cell phone rang in her bedroom. Wearing a towel, she padded down the hall to answer it. "Hello?"

"Hi, it's Tess. Something's happened and I thought you should know about it."

Recognizing the sober tone in Tess's voice, Jocelyn sat down on the edge of her bed. "What is it?"

"Ben Cohen was released yesterday. Apparently, there was mix-up with the warrant they used to search his apartment. A couple of officers crossed wires and they each thought the other had the warrant, and they ended up using one that was meant for someone else."

"Oh, no."

"You might want to go and see Dr. Knight. You want me to call his penthouse?"

"Yes. Tell him not to go out, and that I'm on my way."

Jocelyn threw off the towel and got dressed.

Fifteen minutes later, she was in her car on her way to his place, when her phone rang again. "Yeah?"

"It's Tess. I've been trying his penthouse, and there's no answer. I called the hospital but he's not working today. I haven't been able to get in touch with him, Jo. I hope everything's all right."

A cold chill spurted through her. "Keep trying. Maybe he's out on the terrace or in the shower or something. I'm near his place now. I'll call you when I know something."

She parked, holstered her gun, and dashed into the lobby. "Briggs, is Dr. Knight at home?" she asked the security guard.

"No, Ms. Mackenzie. He's gone for a run. Left about a half hour ago."

"Thanks." She pushed through the revolving door and called Tess again. "He's gone for a run. I'm going to look for him, but you keep trying his penthouse in case we don't cross paths. Tell him to lock his door and not to move until I get there, and call me if you reach him.''

Jocelyn flipped her phone closed and slid it into her pocket. She started running down the street toward the park which had been his regular route before he'd hired her. She was glad she'd worn her sneakers.

The sun warmed her head and shoulders. She worked up a sweat, running in her jeans and blazer, but all she cared about was finding Donovan.

She reached the park and shaded her eyes. She scanned the crowds of people on rollerblades and walking their dogs. There were lots of runners on the paths, but no sign of Donovan.

Then she spotted someone sitting on the ground a distance away, leaning against a tree in the shade, fiddling with a sprig of grass. It was him. A cry of relief spilled from her lips. *Thank God.*

She perused the surroundings, looking for any suspicious-looking characters, and approached.

His gaze shot up. His face paled when she came to a stop in front of him. ''Jocelyn, what are you doing here?''

She had to work hard to catch her breath. She wiped her forehead with the back of a hand. ''I'm so glad I found you.''

He squinted up at her for a few seconds. ''Why?''

''Something's happened. Ben Cohen was released yesterday. You're not safe.''

He said nothing for a few seconds. ''I see.''

''I need to escort you back to your place.''

Donovan stared up at Jocelyn's beautiful dark eyes and full lips, her cheeks flushed from the heat, and wondered how it was possible he could still be so completely in love with her after the way they'd parted three weeks ago.

Between now and then, he'd flip-flopped between feeling furious with her one minute, to picking up the phone and dialing her number to ask her out the next, only to hang up before it rang. He hadn't been able to think of anything but her.

Damn, he'd thought she had come here for personal reasons. He'd thought he was finally going to be able to hold her in his arms again, but she was only here because of his stalker. He'd thought wrong, like he'd been wrong about everything else where she was concerned.

Rising to his feet, he tried not to look at her gorgeous face or the way her jeans clung to her long, sexy legs. If he was ever going to feel normal again, he was going to have to forget about her and convince himself that she'd been right. That what they'd had at the lake hadn't been real.

This was the real Jocelyn. All business. No heart.

"That's fine," he said coolly. "I'll go with you for now, but I think—because we were personally involved—it would be best if I hired someone else to be my bodyguard. You understand, I hope." If he was going to protect himself from falling under her spell again, he couldn't even consider hiring her and inviting her back into his home.

Her lips parted. With surprise? Or was it anguish? If it was anguish, it could be no worse than what he'd suffered when she'd insisted on ending things between them. He would not let himself feel guilty about it.

"All right, let's go this way." She recovered

quickly from whatever she'd been feeling. Always the professional, he thought bitterly.

Keeping her eyes on the path and the people approaching them from any side, Jocelyn walked beside Donovan. They didn't talk. He knew she was focused on what she was doing, and he, to be frank, couldn't have made his mouth work if he tried. He just wanted this to be over.

They approached his building and waited to cross the street. All of a sudden, from out of nowhere, a shot fired past Donovan's head and chiseled a piece of brick out of the building behind him. He instinctively ducked behind a telephone pole. Jocelyn put her arm around him and shielded him with her body, just like she'd done the last time. People on the street were screaming and running. His heart hammered inside his chest.

Another shot blasted by and missed.

"He's not giving up!" Jocelyn, holding her gun in her hand, looked around for better cover.

Donovan peeked out.

"Stay back!" she shouted.

"He's there!"

"Where?"

Donovan peaked out again. "Around the side of my building. He's pointing his gun at us."

Jocelyn leaned out, just as a bullet hit the telephone pole. Wood splintered next to her face. Seizing an opportunity, she fired at Cohen and miraculously knocked his gun out of his hand. Donovan heard Cohen groan with pain, then saw him bolt.

"He's running!" Donovan sprinted out into the street to go after him.

"Donovan, wait!" Jocelyn followed.

Sirens began to wail somewhere in the distance, but Donovan wasn't stopping. He had the chance to catch Cohen now, and he couldn't wait for the cops.

He chased Cohen down the alley and across a back street. Jocelyn's footfalls tapped the ground not far behind him. He knew she had her gun, and Cohen was unarmed. He wasn't giving up now. He leaped over a garbage can.

He was gaining on Cohen. The guy wasn't a runner.

A minute later, Donovan hurled himself through the air and tackled Cohen from behind, into a pile of wooden crates in another alley. He felt his arm scrape against something; his jaw cracked against the back of Cohen's head, and he tasted blood in his mouth.

Cohen scrambled beneath him to get away, but the sound of a gun cocking next to his head made him freeze.

"Hold it right there," Jocelyn said, both hands on her gun, her legs braced apart. "Move one muscle and you'll be leaving here in a body bag."

Donovan took one look at her—tough as nails—and backed off Cohen, who raised his hands in the air. Just then, a cop car skidded to a halt on the street at the end of the alley and a swarm of uniformed officers came bounding around the corner. Donovan wiped his bloody lip with a hand.

"Hey, Ms. Mackenzie," one of the cops said, just before he grabbed Cohen and cuffed him. "Good work."

She lowered her weapon. "It was Dr. Knight who did most of the work, Charlie." Her shoulders rose and fell with a deep intake of breath as she looked at Donovan. "Are you all right?"

He inspected the blood on his hand. "I'll live."

She stared at him, then something in her face changed. The tough-as-nails persona disappeared, and a softness took its place—along with a few tears spilling over her cheeks.

Donovan was breathing hard. So was she. God, he loved her, still.

Jocelyn took three long, fast strides toward him and threw her arms around his neck.

The whole world disappeared around them. Donovan didn't care what was happening to Cohen, he was barely aware of the cops reading the guy his rights. All that mattered was Jocelyn, here in his arms, shuddering with tears and weeping onto his shoulder.

"It's over," he said, stroking her hair. "He's in custody now."

She shook her head against him and sniffled. "That's not why I'm crying. I do this stuff all the time."

He couldn't help laughing. "Then why *are* you crying?"

She looked up at him. Her face was wet and her nose was running. "Because I was afraid I was going to lose you, and I'd never get the chance to tell you how sorry I was."

A warning voice whispered in his head. Maybe she was sorry for not preventing the shooting. Maybe she was sorry for hurting him at the cabin. He didn't want to let himself hope that she might regret saying goodbye....

"Sorry for what?" he asked, despite himself.

The officer named Charlie appeared beside them.

"I'm going to need statements from the both of you."

Donovan and Jocelyn stepped apart. Jocelyn wiped under her nose and quickly collected herself, then began to explain what had happened, as well as the fact that Cohen's gun had flown out of his hand back at Donovan's building and needed to be picked up. The officer had some questions for Donovan, too, then he closed his notebook and said he'd be in touch.

Donovan and Jocelyn stood in the alley, alone at last. Neither of them said anything for a moment or two.

"You okay?" Donovan asked, wishing they hadn't been interrupted before. Jocelyn had been in his arms. He wanted her back.

It wasn't going to happen, however. Not now. The moment had passed, and he wasn't sure what was going on anymore. She was staring at the ground, looking like a tough E.P.P. again.

"You want to go back to my place for a drink?" he asked, not sure where this was going to lead, but wanting to try anyway. "You're off duty now, and I sure as hell could use a beer. I've never apprehended a stalker before." He held up his hand and made it quiver.

He managed to get a smile out of her at least. "Sure. I'd love a beer."

She said yes.

Elation flowed through him.

The very next second, his gut twisted into knots as he smiled down at her and comprehended how much of his future happiness depended on the next half hour of his life.

Twelve

Donovan pulled his key from his shoe wallet and unlocked the door to his penthouse.

"Wait." Jocelyn touched his arm and held him back. "Let me go first and check things out. You never know."

Donovan exhaled deeply. She was dedicated to her work, and he respected her for it, even when it got in the way of his hopes to make this drink personal rather than professional.

He waited by the door while she disarmed the alarm and checked his penthouse for God knew what. A short time later, she came sauntering out of his bedroom.

What he wouldn't give to see her sauntering out of there every morning for the rest of his life....

Brushing those hopes aside, he smiled. "Everything okay?"

"Yeah, it looks fine. How about that beer?"

"Coming right up. Make yourself comfortable." It felt strange, treating her like a guest when she'd been his roommate not that long ago.

Donovan went to change into a pair of jeans and a clean shirt, then went to the kitchen and pulled two cold ones out of the fridge and twisted off the caps. He poured them into a couple of mugs and started heading down the hall.

He stopped in his tracks, however, when he heard his Eric Clapton CD playing. Memories of those early nights with Jocelyn came flooding back. He remembered discovering for the first time something of the real woman beneath the suit and the tough girl image. He remembered the way she'd smiled when she'd heard those songs.

He swallowed hard over his anxiety, his fear that today might end the same as that pivotal night at the cabin—when an argument and a breakup had wedged them apart.

"Here you go." He entered the living room and handed her mug to her. "Cheers. Here's to Cohen behind bars again."

"I'll drink to that." They clinked glasses and sipped their beer.

"Have a seat," Donovan said, feeling awkward and out of his element, trying to be casual when all he really wanted to do was take Jocelyn into his arms and kiss every inch of her.

That would probably scare her off, though—to put it mildly—and at this point, he was more than willing to go slow and cool his jets, like she'd asked him to do, that final night at the cabin.

Damn, he'd stand on his head for a week if it

would change her mind about ending their relationship.

She sat down and kicked off her shoes, then tucked her jean clad legs up under her. "Donovan, I'm glad you invited me here, because I really wanted to talk to you today."

He cleared his throat nervously. "About Cohen?"

For a moment she stared at him. "No. I...I know that's why I went looking for you at the park, but the truth is, I was planning to come and see you before I knew about his release."

Donovan remembered how he'd felt when he'd first looked up at her in the park, how he'd hoped she was there just for him. Then the disappointment...

He waited in silence for her to continue.

She lowered her gaze, drawing little circles on his upholstery with the tip of her index finger. "I...I've missed you."

All his nerve endings began to quake and buzz.

"The past few weeks have been hell," she said. "I haven't been able to stop thinking about you, and I hate the way things ended between us. That week at the cabin was the best week of my life, and I totally screwed it up."

"You didn't screw it up, Jocelyn," he said gently, covering her hand with his.

"Yes, I did." Her voice quavered, but she spoke with a candid resonance, looking him directly in the eye. "I'm sorry for being such a coward."

He sat there, dumbfounded, bewildered and shaken. "What are you saying?"

"I'm saying that I was an idiot. I was afraid to love you because of the things I remember about my father and Tom. I was afraid of getting hurt, but walking away from you hurt even more. I want to go back to what we had. I only hope that you can forgive me for causing you pain, and I hope you still..." She lowered her face.

Donovan inched closer to her and cradled her chin in his hand. "You hope I still what?"

Her eyes were wet and bloodshot as she gazed up at him. "I hope you still want me."

His entire being heated from the inside out. Everything was pulsing with joy and excitement and profound relief. How could she even doubt if for a minute?

"I never stopped wanting you, Jocelyn. I wanted you the first second I saw you, standing at my door with that serious glare in your eyes, just like I want you now."

She blinked up at him, all woman—vulnerable, feminine. Her lips were moist and parted and a pulse of arousal began to throb in his loins. He took her face in his hands and covered her mouth with his own.

Jocelyn wrapped her arms around his neck and he pulled her into his embrace, deepening the kiss and letting his hands slide down the soft curves of her body. How many nights had he lain awake dreaming of this? How many nights had he wished she would come to him and tell him she wanted to go back to what they were when they were together?

Yet none of those dreams could compare to the exhilarating flesh and blood feel of her in his arms now, her mouth tasting deliciously of beer and her hair smelling of citrus. He couldn't get enough. He didn't think he would ever get enough....

"I love you," he whispered in her ear, nibbling at her lobe and feeling her writhe with rapture and delight. "You're the only woman who has ever filled the hole in my life, Jocelyn—the sense of emptiness, from never feeling ready to let anyone in."

"I don't know what I did to deserve you."

"You were just you."

He took her mouth again with a wild intensity, and drank in the luscious flavor of her whole being.

"I promise I won't get spooked this time," she said, tipping her head back as he dropped open kisses upon her neck. "These weeks away from you gave me time to understand that what we had wasn't just an infatuation. I needed time to think about everything, because as you know, I'm not impulsive. But I'm here now, Donovan, and I'm yours. Completely."

He drew back to look into her eyes. "You're sure about that?"

"I've never been more sure of anything."

He kissed her again, long and slow, then sat back. "Will you stay here for a second?"

"Sure." She watched him curiously as he kissed her on the forehead and left the room.

He went to the safe in his bedroom and turned the knob left, twenty-four, then right, sixty-eight, then left again to five and back to zero. He couldn't go fast enough. Damn, his hands were shaking!

Finally the safe clicked open and he reached inside for the little velvet box he'd been saving his entire life. His heart was racing.

He paused a moment and took a deep breath, feeling his world shift. Everything was changing. He slipped the box into his pocket.

Donovan walked down the hall and returned to the living room, where Jocelyn was waiting on the sofa, all smiles, looking flushed and beautiful, like an angel from heaven. He slowly made his way to her and knelt at her feet.

His heart was pounding against his ribs. He'd never been so nervous about anything in his life.

He took her hands in his and labored to keep his voice steady and controlled. "You're the one, Jocelyn. I know it as clearly as I know my own soul. You're the one I want to spend my life with, the one I want to grow old with, and I promise I will make you happy forever, and I will never, ever leave you, if only you'll say yes."

Her eyes were sparkling. She began to smile. "Yes to what?"

"Yes to marrying me. I didn't propose properly last time. This time, I'm doing it right." He reached into his pocket, withdrew the box and opened it before her. The diamond ring glittered magically. "This was my mother's. She left it to me in her will. She said it signified everlasting love, and that it would represent her love for me even after she was gone, and that she hoped I would pass it on to my own children. It means a lot to me. Will you wear it, and give it to our child some day?"

Jocelyn covered her mouth with trembling fingers and stared down at the one-and-a-half carat, pear-shaped diamond. "It's the most beautiful ring I've ever seen, Donovan." She took it out of the box and tried it on. "It fits perfectly."

Donovan got up off his knees to sit beside her again. He touched her cheek lovingly. "Meant to be, I guess."

She began to nod. "I think you're right. I feel good about this. I feel *really* good about it."

He exhaled a long sigh of contentment, then kissed her again, tenderly and passionately, stroking her hair and her shoulders and glorying in the feel of her body next to his. "I feel good, too. I'll always feel good with you in my life, Jocelyn. I hope you don't want a long engagement."

She smiled seductively. "I'll marry you tomorrow if you can get the time off."

A swell of arousal moved through him at the beguiling expression on her face and the sexy, silky sound of her voice. "Tomorrow might be a little difficult. How about the day after?"

"What's so important tomorrow?" she asked, laying teasing little kisses on his chin and neck. The feel of her wet lips on his skin sent a message to his nether regions, and he began to rise to this tantalizing occasion.

"Tomorrow I'm helping you move in here," he replied. "That is, if you *want* to live here."

"Of course I do." Her voice became serious. "It was your parents' place, Donovan, and look what they created while they lived here." She touched her warm palm to his cheek. "We have a lot to look forward to, don't we? But for now, I only want one thing."

"And what's that?"

Her eyes glimmered with desire. She pulled off her shirt to reveal a red, lace teddy. "I want you to carry me to your bedroom, so I can thank you for bringing out the woman in me."

His hunger for his new fiancée intensified. He

rubbed his nose up against hers. ''We'll get there faster if we run.''

She laughed and leaped off the sofa. ''As long as you promise to go slow when we get there.''

Desire burned through his body at the idea of making love to her slowly, for the rest of the day and long into the night, in the bedroom that would become theirs together, forever. ''I wouldn't have it any other way.''

*   *   *   *   *

COMING NEXT MONTH

#1519 SCENES OF PASSION—Suzanne Brockmann

Maggie Stanton knew something was missing from her picture-perfect life, and when she ran into her high school buddy Michael Stone, she knew just what it was. The former bad boy had grown into a charismatic man who was everything Maggie had ever dreamed of. But if they were to have a future together, Maggie would have to learn to trust him.

#1520 CINDERELLA'S MILLIONAIRE—Katherine Garbera

Dynasties: The Barones

Love was the last thing on widower Joseph Barone's mind…until he was roped into escorting pastry chef Holly Fitzgerald to a media interview. The brooding millionaire had built an impenetrable wall around his heart, but delectable Holly was pure temptation. He needed her—in his bed and in his life—but was he ready to risk his heart again?

#1521 IN BED WITH THE ENEMY—Kathie DeNosky

Lone Star Country Club

ATF agent Cole Yardley didn't believe women belonged in the field, fighting crime, but then a gun-smuggling investigation brought him and FBI agent Elise Campbell together. Though he'd intended to ignore Elise, Cole soon found himself surrendering to the insatiable hunger she stirred in him.…

#1522 EXPECTING THE COWBOY'S BABY—Charlene Sands

An old flame came roaring back to life when Cassie Munroe went home for her brother's wedding and ran into Jake Griffin, her high school ex. The boy who'd broken her heart was gone, and in his place was one sinfully sexy man. They wound up sharing an unforgettable night of passion that would change Cassie's life forever, for now she was pregnant with Jake's baby!

#1523 CHEROKEE DAD—Sheri WhiteFeather

Desperate to keep her nephew safe, Heather Richmond turned to Michael Elk, the man she'd left behind eighteen months ago. Michael still touched her soul in a way no other man ever had, and she couldn't resist the seductive promises in his eyes. She only hoped he would forgive her once he discovered her secret.…

#1524 THE GENTRYS: CAL—Linda Conrad

When Cal Gentry went home to his family ranch to recover from the accident that killed his wife, he found Isabella de la Cruz on his doorstep. The mysterious beauty needed protecting…and soon found a sense of security in Cal's arms. Then, as things heated up between them, Cal vowed to convince Isabella to accept not only his protection, but his heart, as well.

SDCNM0603